But as for you, ye thought evil against me;
but God meant it unto good, to bring to pass,
as it is this day, to save much people alive.
   –Genesis 50:20

To all of the men, women and four-legged heroes
who fight for justice on a daily basis.
Thank you for your service.

Luke cleared his throat. "You ready?"

"Sure."

He and Bruno followed Sophie to the front door of her unit.

Which was cracked open.

She gasped and stepped back.

"That's not supposed to be open, I'm guessing?" Luke whispered.

"No."

"Stand back against the wall. Bruno, stay." In the blink of an eye, the dog's demeanor changed at Luke's command. His ears went up and he was in instant work mode, waiting for the next order.

A loud crash came from the bedroom area and Luke headed down the hallway. "NYPD! Come out of the room! Hands where I can see them! Now!"

TRUE BLUE K-9 UNIT:

These police officers fight for justice
with the help of their brave canine partners

Lynette Eason is a bestselling, award-winning author who makes her home in South Carolina with her husband and two teenage children. She enjoys traveling, spending time with her family and teaching at various writing conferences around the country. She is a member of Romance Writers of America and American Christian Fiction Writers. Lynette can often be found online interacting with her readers. You can find her at Facebook.com/lynette.eason and on Twitter, @lynetteeason.

Books by Lynette Eason

Love Inspired Suspense

True Blue K-9 Unit
Justice Mission

Wrangler's Corner
The Lawman Returns
Rodeo Rescuer
Protecting Her Daughter
Classified Christmas Mission
Vanished in the Night
Holiday Amnesia

Military K-9 Unit
Explosive Force

Classified K-9 Unit
Bounty Hunter

Visit the Author Profile page at Harlequin.com for more titles.

JUSTICE MISSION

LYNETTE EASON

❤ HARLEQUIN® LOVE INSPIRED® SUSPENSE

Special thanks and acknowledgment are given to Lynette Eason for her contribution to the True Blue K-9 Unit miniseries.

Recycling programs
for this product may
not exist in your area.

LOVE INSPIRED BOOKS

ISBN-13: 978-1-335-67887-4

Justice Mission

www.Harlequin.com

Printed in U.S.A.

ONE

Sophie Walters stood back to count the rows of chairs and relished the thought of the upcoming graduation ceremony that would take place shortly in the auditorium near the NYC K-9 Command Unit headquarters where she worked in Forest Hills, Queens. Today, several new four-legged recruits and their handlers would graduate and join the force in keeping New York City safe.

The unit was made up of officers who handled dogs with a variety of specialties. While based out of their office in Queens, the officers were assigned to divisions of the NYPD throughout the five boroughs of New York City where needed.

As the administrative assistant to Chief Jordan Jameson, who headed up the NYC K-9 Command Unit, Sophie had a wide range of duties, but she'd be the first to admit, she loved the graduation ceremonies most.

Hands down, she loved her job and took pride in the fact that she was very good at it. Something the chief often praised her for. "You have an eye for detail and organization, Sophie," he'd said on more than one occasion. "I don't know what this place would do without you."

If only he knew how hard she'd worked to develop that eye for detail. Sophie smiled, her heart grateful for the man who'd taken a chance on a young green college graduate three years ago.

A thud from the back of the auditorium drew her attention to the left-hand corner and she frowned. "Hello? Is someone there?"

Stillness settled over the large room. When nothing more happened and no one announced their presence, she returned her attention to the ceremony preparations.

Something was wrong. Off. But what?

A little prickle at the base of her neck sent shivers down her spine and she turned to assess the area once more. The auditorium chairs sat empty. She'd unlocked all of the doors in case she had some early arrivals, but the place was quiet for now. Quiet as a tomb. Now, why would she think that? There'd been no more strange noises and nothing that should spark her unease. But she couldn't help feeling like someone was watching.

But why?

And who?

"No one," she muttered. "Quit jumping at shadows." But something still nagged at her.

Sophie scanned the stage trying to put her finger on it. Six chairs aligned just right on the artificial turf. The podium with the chief's notes for his presentation within easy reach, the mic was at exactly the right height, the graduation certificates were laid out in alphabetical order on the table…

The table.

She huffed. She'd placed everything on it without putting the black cloth on. Where was her mind this morning?

Definitely on her brother and the attention-stealing phone call she'd received last night. He'd called to tell her he was quitting college to join the Marines.

Seriously? He was nineteen years old. "What does a nineteen-year-old know?" she muttered. Nothing. Which was probably why he wanted to join the Marines.

But who was she to say it was a bad idea? He was right. They were different people with different lives, but she'd been ten years old when their mother had left and she'd taken on the role of mother figure for Trey. For the past fourteen years, he'd looked at her that way. And now he wanted her to just step aside while he made an important decision without discussing it? A small part of her reminded herself that he was technically an adult.

"But I'm the one who attended the parent/teacher conferences when Dad couldn't get off work," she muttered. "I'm the one who fixed his snacks and washed his clothes and held him when he got his heart broken by the girl who dumped him his sophomore year of high school."

Stop it. Let it go for now and do your job.

Sophie removed the black tablecloth from the supply closet in the hallway, then hurried back toward the auditorium, her mind tuned in to the graduation details now.

She pushed through the auditorium door to the right of the stage and stumbled to a halt. A man in a baseball cap and sunglasses stood next to the podium with Chief Jameson's red remarks folder open.

"Excuse me, what are you doing?" Sophie asked. He'd frozen for a slight second when she entered but closed the folder as she strode toward him. Her low heels clicked on the wooden steps and rang through the empty room. She approached him, intent on rescuing Jordan's notes if need be. "The ceremony doesn't start for another forty-five minutes. Did you need help with something?"

"Ah. No." He turned toward her. "Thanks, but—" He kept his head lowered and she couldn't make out a thing about his features.

A little niggle of fear curled in her belly and she remembered the loud noise, the feeling of someone watching her. She stopped so suddenly, she actually slid a couple more inches on the wood floor. Had he been in the auditorium the whole time? Watching her? Waiting for her to leave so he could look through Jordan's folder?

No, of course not. She was being silly.

"But?" She encouraged him to finish his statement even while she could feel his laser-like stare shooting at her from behind the dark glasses. "Were you looking for something in the folder? It's just notes for a speech."

Once again unease shook her. Maybe she wasn't being so silly after all. Something wasn't right with this.

Get away from him.

Goose bumps pebbled her arms, and she turned to run. His left hand shot out and closed around her right bicep as his right hand came up, fingers wrapped around the grip of a gun. Sophie screamed when he placed the barrel of the weapon against her head. "Shut up," he hissed. "Cooperate, and I might let you live."

A gun. He had a gun pointed at her temple. "What are you doing? Why are you doing this? I don't have any money on me." Her shaky voice tumbled from trembling lips. She clamped them down, fighting for control.

His grip tightened. "Go."

Go? "Where?"

"Out the side door and to the parking lot. Now."

"Why don't you go, and I'll forget this ever happened?"

"Too late for that. You're coming with me. Now, move!"

"You're *kidnapping* me?" She squeezed the words out, trying to breathe through her terror.

"I said shut up! I'm not going to prison because of you!"

Still keeping his fingers tight around her upper arm, he gave her a hard shove and Sophie stumbled down the steps of the podium, his grip the only thing that kept her from landing on her face.

Her captor aimed her toward the door, and she had no choice but to follow. Heart thundering in her chest, her gaze jerked around the empty room. No help there. Maybe someone would be in the parking lot?

He pushed the silver bar and the steel door swung out. The gun moved from her head to dig into the center of her back, propelling her out onto the asphalt. His other hand snagged the loose bun at the nape of her neck, yanking her head sideways.

She cried out even while she squinted against the glare of the bright morning sun. Normally, her penchant for being early averted a lot of things that could go wrong and usurp her daily schedule. Today, it had placed her in the hands of a dangerous man—and an empty parking lot in Jackson Heights. Where was everyone?

Think, Sophie, think!

A K-9 SUV turned in and she caught a glimpse of the driver. Officer Luke Hathaway sat behind the wheel of the SUV. "Luke!"

"Shut up!" Her captor jerked her toward a

brown sedan with a glance over his shoulder. His grip didn't loosen until he got to the driver's side of the vehicle. "Open the door!"

No way. With a burst of strength, she jabbed back with her left elbow. A yell burst from him along with a string of curses. She slipped from his grip for a brief second until he slammed his weapon against the side of her head.

She screamed as pain raced through her and stars danced, threatening to send her into the approaching blackness. Her captor opened the door and shoved her inside before she could gather her wits. She landed halfway on the middle console and halfway in the passenger seat with the gearshift digging into her hip. Head pounding, heart thudding, the blackness faded and she cried out once again as he gave her another hard push, forcing her awkwardly into the passenger seat.

The door slammed.

"Sophie!"

She heard Luke call her name and tried to ignore the nausea climbing into the back of her throat as she grabbed for the passenger-door handle. Her captor shot out a hand and grasped her by the hair. "Stay still, or I'll shoot you now."

The car roared to life and spun out of the lot.

Luke stared in horror as he realized he'd just witnessed Sophie being kidnapped. He pressed the gas and the SUV shot after the fleeing sedan.

Bruno, his K-9 partner seated safely in his spot in the back, barked. "I know, boy," Luke murmured to the German shepherd. "I'm going after her." Luke grabbed his radio. "Officer needs backup. I have 207 in progress. Repeat, kidnapping in progress. Sophie Walters, Chief Jameson's assistant, is the victim. In pursuit of a brown Buick sedan, license plate Eddie-Larry-Peter-four-seven-five-eight. Closing in on pursuit position." He gave his location and kept a watch for other cars and innocent bystanders.

Unfortunately, Sophie's kidnapper didn't have any such concern. The man swerved to the right and around a parked car, then up on the sidewalk. People scattered like ants. A trash can bounced off the windshield and Luke yanked the wheel to the left to avoid it. Two police cruisers fell in behind him.

Bruno barked again. Luke knew how the dog felt. "Going as fast as I can, buddy." He lifted the radio once again. "Just hit Ninety-Fourth, heading straight for Roosevelt Avenue. Need someone to head him off." Luke wanted to gun the engine, but he didn't dare. The streets weren't packed, but enough innocent people were there to keep him careful.

In and out of traffic, the man drove, even in the wrong lane several times. Luke stayed with him. Backup stayed behind Luke. "He just took a right on Broadway. I'm guessing he's heading for the

Brooklyn-Queens Expressway. Repeat, he's heading toward the BQE."

Luke received confirmation that officers were en route to that area. "Come on, come on. Slow down. Run out of gas. Anything."

But the man kept going. Fortunately, Luke's siren caught people's attention so that they moved out of the way. Sure enough, the man merged from Broadway onto the BQE. "Heading in the direction of the Triborough Bridge. Somebody stop this guy, but be careful, he's got a kidnapping victim with him. Sophie Walters. Civilian employee of the NYPD."

"Copy that," came the response.

The driver continued his game of dodge and somehow managed to avoid crashing into anything.

Luke followed, staying far enough behind so as not to miss a sudden turn, but close enough not to lose the guy. With each turn, Luke gave the directions, knowing backup would try to cut the guy off. Unfortunately, with no clear destination, he couldn't give them clear enough direction.

Where was this guy going? How much longer could he drive like this without killing someone? Tension threaded Luke's shoulders with knots. The kidnapper took another left, heading for one of the more crowded areas of Astoria. The potential for someone to get hurt had just jumped astronomically. Luke requested the area be cleared immediately but knew it wouldn't be in time.

The fleeing suspect missed a city bus by a fraction of an inch and Luke barely squeaked past it himself. A young man on a delivery bike slammed into the side of a parked car in his desperate attempt to keep from barreling in front of the speeding sedan. Briefly, Luke hoped the poor cyclist hadn't broken anything.

Luke braked hard when the sedan swerved. Tires squealing, it headed straight for a fruit stand on the corner. Screams echoed. People ran. The vehicle rammed into the stand, sending produce flying and the owner diving out of the way. Luke screeched to a stop and threw the car into Park. He bolted from the driver's seat and hit the remote button that opened Bruno's area. Bruno leaped out to follow as Luke raced toward the wrecked vehicle in time to see the driver grab Sophie by the arm and pull her from the car.

"Stop! NYPD!" Luke dodged the fleeing crowd and fought his way toward Sophie. "Sophie!"

"Luke!" Her terrified scream spurred him faster. Bruno stayed with him. Backup was right behind him, adding their commands to stop.

Sophie struggled against her captor, and he yanked her hard. She stumbled. Luke closed in, reaching for her. And then the man shoved her away from him. Sophie let out another scream as she flew toward Luke, barreling into him, knocking him off balance.

He fell back, tripping over Bruno, who yelped and scrambled to move out of the way. Luke's back hit the sidewalk with a breath-stealing thud. Sophie landed on top of him and the last of his air left his lungs. From the corner of his eye, he caught sight of the man disappearing into the nearest building. Officers pounded after him.

Gasping, Luke rolled. "You okay?" he wheezed to Sophie.

She groaned and pressed a hand to her head.

Luke staggered to his feet, then helped her up as other officers rushed past them, going after the kidnapper. Two more slowed as though to check on them and Luke waved them on. They took off and Sophie leaned heavily against him. Bystanders crowded around, asking if they were okay while he held her, trying to discern where she was hurt.

Her usually neat bun had fallen, and her long brown hair lay in disarray across her shoulders. He brushed the strands from her eyes and she blinked up at him. "Talk to me, Sophie. You're okay, right?"

"Yes. I… Yes," she whispered. "I… I think so."

He caught sight of the blood on the side of her head. "Wait a minute. You're not okay. We need to get you checked out."

"No, it's all right. Just give me a minute to catch my breath and let my head stop spinning."

"You're hurt. You need a hospital."

She touched her head with a wince. "No, what I *need* is to get back to the auditorium. We've got a graduation that needs to go on."

"Sophie—"

"I'm serious. That guy was only after me because I saw him messing with Chief Jameson's folder on the podium. I want to know what he was doing and if he left something behind that would tell us who he is." She grimaced. "Then you can go after him again."

For a moment Luke could only stare at her. She'd been kidnapped, knocked in the head, driven through the city at breakneck speed, and all she could think about was getting back to see what the guy had been up to? "You're amazing."

She blinked. "No. I'm mad."

"All right. Let's head back to the auditorium, then. While we're riding, you can fill me in on the details."

"Thank you."

Luke caught Bruno's leash, and Sophie followed him—limping slightly—back to his Tahoe, where she climbed into the front seat and fastened her seat belt. Luke settled behind the driver's seat and held the radio to his mouth. "Any sign of the guy who kidnapped Sophie?"

"That's a negative." The voice came back at

him through the speaker. "He disappeared after officers chased him through the store. We're still canvassing the area."

"Ten-four."

By the time Luke pulled into the parking lot at the auditorium, Sophie had filled him in on everything that had led to her kidnapping. And Luke was inclined to agree with her. This wasn't just some random snatching. The man at the podium had had a goal—and Luke was itching to figure out what it was.

Another car pulled into the lot.

"Everyone is arriving," she said. "We need to make this fast so we can stay on schedule."

"Sophie—"

But she was already out of the car and hurrying—limping—toward the door she'd been forced from about thirty minutes ago.

"The ceremony can start late, you know," he murmured to her back. With a sigh, he let Bruno out and they followed after Sophie. Inside, he found her surrounded by other officers concerned with her safety. She repeated all of her "I'm shaken up but fine" reassurances until they accepted the answer even if they didn't fully believe it.

"Is she really okay?" Officer Zach Jameson asked. A fellow officer with the NYC K-9 Command Unit, Zach was also the youngest brother to Jordan Jameson, the chief. The family resemblance was startling with his brown hair and blue eyes. Luke noted Carter and Noah, the other two Jameson brothers, standing nearby with their K-9s seated at their sides.

"She says she is," Luke said with a frown. "That's all I have to go on."

The Jamesons had made law enforcement their family business and all had arrived to attend the ceremony, then get back to work. Officer Finn Gallagher, another K-9 Command Unit member, stood nearby, green eyes watching. Usually the jovial, outgoing jokester of the group, he now sported tight features and a tense jaw.

Luke nodded to Chief Jameson's wife, sitting in the front row and glancing at her watch. "Is Katie all right? She looks a little pale."

Jordan's wife had her blond hair in a French braid that fell over her right shoulder. Her blue eyes continued to bounce between her watch and the door her husband should have entered at least fifteen minutes ago.

"I noticed that, too, but when I asked, she said she was fine, just feeling a little under the weather and that she and Jordan had an errand to run after the ceremony so she thought she'd just come watch."

"She's always been crazy about the dogs," Luke said. "And Jordan likes having her here." He glanced around. "Speaking of Jordan, where is he?"

Zach shrugged, blue eyes narrowed as he watched his sister-in-law. "Katie's wondering that, too. He's usually here by now, going over his notes or shaking hands—and paws—with the soon-to-be new graduates."

Sophie broke free of her concerned friends and headed for the stage. Luke and Bruno followed her up the steps and to the podium. "Where's Jordan?" Luke asked. "Did he say anything about running late?"

"No. At least not before I was snatched." Her hand shook slightly as she reached for the red folder. "Let's see what my kidnapper found so fascinating about Jordan's notes." She flipped the folder open and an envelope fell to the floor. Frowning, she retrieved it, slipped a finger under the flap and pulled out the paper inside. Her eyes scanned it and she gasped, the color leeching from her cheeks.

"Sophie?" Luke hurried the last few steps to her side, thinking the knock on her head had finally caught up to her. "Are you okay? You need to sit down?"

"No." She stared at the letter, and Luke frowned. No, she wasn't okay, or no, she didn't need to sit down? He stepped behind her to read over her shoulder.

I can't go on anymore. Please make sure Katie is taken care of. Jordan Jameson.

TWO

Sophie fought to catch her breath. "This reads like a—a—" She couldn't say it.

"Suicide note," Luke finished for her, his brows drawn tightly over the bridge of his nose.

"No," she whispered. "He wouldn't." Her eyes met Katie's. Jordan's wife frowned even though she was too far away to know what was going on.

But one thing was certain. Jordan had too much to live for to take his own life. Just last week Katie had walked into headquarters to meet Jordan for lunch and then suddenly made a mad dash past Sophie's desk and into the restroom. Concerned, Sophie had followed only to hear Katie throwing up.

"Are you all right?" she'd asked when the woman had finally emerged from the stall and finished with the sink.

Katie had checked under each stall, then turned to Sophie and grinned. "We're alone, so I can tell you that I'm absolutely perfect."

At first, Sophie could only blink. Then gasp. "You're pregnant!"

"Shh!" Katie had held a finger to her lips. "I haven't told anyone yet."

"What about Jordan?"

"He knows, but no one else. We're kind of in shock, but it's thrilling and we're really just savoring the moment, you know? We plan to tell everyone soon. Probably after the first trimester."

"Good for you." Sophie had hugged her friend. "I won't tell a soul. What did Jordan say when you told him?"

"He was over-the-moon excited."

"Wouldn't what? Sophie? Hello?" Noah Jameson's voice brought Sophie back to the present.

She blinked away the memory and her gaze lifted to meet Luke's, then slid around the others who'd gathered in front of her, their expressions confused and slightly wary. All except Noah's. She never could read him.

Sophie passed him the note. Noah read it, his expression shutting down even more, then passed it to his brothers. "You're right. He *wouldn't*."

"No, he *definitely* wouldn't," Zach said, pulling his phone from his pocket. "I'll call him, and he'll straighten this out." They waited in silence as Zach stood and punched in his brother's number, blue eyes narrowed. He ran a hand through his hair and pressed the device to his ear, his ris-

ing tension adding to the thickness already surrounding them all.

Seconds ticked.

"Answer the phone, Jordan," Sophie whispered.

But Zach was already lowering the device. "It
went straight to voice mail."

"No," Sophie said. "That's not possible. He
never turns his phone off. Especially not on a day
like this. Straight to voice mail? That scares me
a little." A *lot*.

"It's scaring Katie, too," Noah said with a
glance at his sister-in-law, who watched them
from her first-row seat in the auditorium. Too far
away to hear the conversation, yet close enough
to know something serious was going on and Sophie knew they were going to have to fill her in.

As though Sophie's gaze compelled her, Katie
stood and walked toward them. Noah met her in
front of the stage. "What is it? You're all acting
weird and being super secretive."

"Can you call Jordan?" Noah asked.

"Why?"

"We need to know where he is and I'm sure if
he's got his phone on the Do Not Disturb setting
for whatever reason, he'll have it programmed so
that you'll ring right through."

A door slammed in the back and laughter
reached them.

"Let's move out of the auditorium," Sophie said.

"People are starting to arrive and we'll have more privacy in the room next door."

She led the way into a room that held three sofas and a couple of chairs. A full kitchen dominated the back wall to allow for catered events. All of this registered in a nanosecond before they surrounded Katie and waited for her to dial Jordan's number.

With a frown, Katie did as requested, listened for a moment, then hung up. "It went straight to voice mail." Her eyes darted from one brother to the next.

Sophie's nerves tightened, and Katie's gaze landed on hers. Sophie knew what her friend was thinking. Jordan never turned off his phone. Ever. And if for some reason, he decided to do so, he'd let someone know in advance. Especially in case Katie needed to reach him.

"He's not answering her either," Noah murmured. "I don't believe this. This isn't good."

"I have the password to his phone, so I can track it," Katie said. "He always wants me to be able to locate him if I need to. I've never used it before. I've never had to."

"Then I'd say this would be a good time to do it," Luke said. "Do you mind seeing what you can find out?"

"Of course." She punched in the digits, then lifted her gaze to meet his and the others who'd gathered around her.

"What is it?" Luke asked. "Can you tell us where he is?"

"Something's wrong. It says his phone's offline, but it shouldn't be. He's never offline." Her eyes narrowed. "I'm starting to get really scared. What's going on?"

Carter shook his head. "We don't know, but I've had enough standing around. I'm going to look for him."

"Me, too," Zach said.

"I'm coming, too." Noah shoved his phone back on his clip and planted his hands on his hips. "But before we run out of here all hasty and unorganized, let's get a plan of action together."

Of course that would be Noah's first thought.

"Wait a minute," Katie said.

They froze.

"I don't understand." Katie crossed her arms. "Can someone please explain to me why you're going to look for Jordan when he should have walked through the door way before now?" Katie asked, her voice containing a slightly hysterical edge. "And then tell me why he would have his phone turned off because if you can't, then something's really, really *wrong*." Worry drew lines across her forehead and at the corners of her mouth. Tears shimmered in her eyes. "I know I keep saying that, but I need to know where he is and if he's okay. And you guys know something you're not telling me. Now, please, *what is it*?"

Sophie bit her lip. "We found a note that seems to indicate he's in trouble. Everyone is getting ready to go search for him."

"What kind of trouble?"

"We're not sure, but we're going to find out," Zach said. He put an arm around his sister-in-law's shoulders. "Let's go over here a second so we can talk."

Noah and Carter joined the two off to the side, and Katie gave a sharp cry. Sophie figured they'd told her the contents of the note. Ignoring the need to rush over and comfort her friend, she turned to the others. "Just so I'm clear, I don't believe Jordan wrote that note for one second, but we can't take the chance that it's not real. We have to act as though he did and that he means it."

Luke nodded. "I agree. But where do we start looking?"

Zach and Katie had returned in time to hear her comment. Katie shook her head, tears streaming down her cheeks. "He wouldn't kill himself. He didn't leave that note!"

"We know," Sophie said. She faced Katie and took her friend's hands. "We don't believe it either. Something else is going on and we're going to find out, okay?"

"Yes. Yes, we are." Katie lifted her chin and swiped her hands over her face.

"The guy who snatched me was messing with

the folder when I walked in," Sophie said. "Maybe he put the note in there."

"If that's the case, then we need to find Jordan immediately," Luke said.

Katie nodded. "Exactly, So, what's the plan?"

"Was Jordan headed straight here when he left this morning?"

"No," she sniffed. "He was going to take Snapper out to the Vanderbilt Parkway and run part of the bike path, then go to headquarters to shower and change before coming over here."

"Vanderbilt Parkway," Luke said. Also known as the Long Island Motor Parkway. A big part of New York's history, it was a great place to run or ride bikes now that automobiles were banned from it—and he knew it was part of Jordan's daily routine. "Then that's where we'll look first."

"We need to check any of his favorite places, as well," Sophie said.

"He had a lot of favorite places," Katie said. "Not all of them are in Queens."

Luke nodded. "Then we're going to need more manpower. Someone call Gavin and fill him in on what's going on."

"Today's his day off," Sophie said, picturing the tall, dark-haired, brown-eyed handler. Gavin Sutherland was another K-9 officer. His Springer spaniel was well-trained to sniff out explosives. And while they may not need Tommy for that reason, she knew as well as Luke did that Gavin would never forgive them if they didn't include him in the search for their boss. "We'll also need to get a BOLO out on Jordan and get his face in front of people as well as notify officers in all the boroughs to be watching for him."

"No," Katie said.

Carter raised a brow. "No?"

"You know Jordan. He'd hate that. There's got to be some other way."

"But we need to find him fast," Noah said. "In order to do that, we need as many eyes looking for him as possible."

"But—"

"They're right, Katie," Sophie said softly. "I'm sorry, but they are. I'd rather live with his anger than something really be wrong and we not pull out all the stops."

"And besides," Luke said, "that guy was messing with the folder. It's very possible he's the one who put that note there. If so, this could be some kind of setup to make it look like Jordan's going to commit suicide. If that's the case, then speed is of the essence before…"

Before he was killed.

No one wanted to say it, but everyone sure thought it.

Katie swiped another tear and a heavy sigh escaped her. She finally shook her head and planted her hands on her hips. "Okay. Fine. You're right.

We need as many people looking for him as we can get."

The brothers nodded.

"All right," Luke said. "I'm going to see if Dani can trace his vehicle."

"Good idea," Sophie said. Danielle Abbott, one of the department's technical analysts would use the GPS attached to the SUV to get a ping on its location.

"Zach," Luke said, "you get the BOLO out." K-9 Officers Brianne Hayes and Tony Knight stepped forward with Finn. Luke turned to Katie. "Can you make up a list of all of Jordan's favorite places and give it to these guys?"

"Of course."

"Once Katie gives you the list," he said to the others, "divide up. Bruno and I have the Vanderbilt Parkway."

"And me," Sophie said. "We can't have the ceremony without Jordan, so we'll just postpone it until he can be here."

"Postpone the ceremony," Luke said, "but you don't need to go. You've just been through a major trauma."

Sophie straightened her shoulders and lifted her chin. "Jordan's my boss, too. I'm as much a part of this department as the rest of you—"

Luke held up a hand. "I'm not saying you're not."

"Good. And I might even be able to identify

the guy in spite of his ballcap and sunglasses. Maybe. So let's not waste any more time debating whether I'm going or not." She headed for the exit, limping slightly.

Luke frowned. "Fine. I'd rather have you with us anyway."

"Thank you," she tossed over her shoulder.

"At least then I'll know you're safe," he muttered.

She grimaced but refused to comment. Instead, she prayed as they raced toward Vanderbilt Parkway. It seemed to take forever to reach it in spite of the sirens that moved traffic out of the way.

Dani had quickly gotten back to them, saying the GPS had been disabled on Jordan's SUV and she wasn't able to get a location on the vehicle.

"What could possibly be going on with him?" Sophie asked. "Jordan wouldn't disable the GPS and he didn't leave that letter, Luke. I think the man who grabbed me did."

"I'd say that's a real possibility, but we have to cover all the bases."

"I know. I'm just saying that I've never seen Jordan so low he'd want to take his own life. Sure, he has struggles, but who doesn't?" She shook her head as she envisioned confronting her brother about his—in her opinion—questionable decision to join the Marines. "But he's not even close to being suicidal." Especially with a baby on the way that he was excited about. But that wasn't her news to share. "There's something else going on and we need to figure out what it is."

"What we need to do is find Jordan and let him tell us."

"Yes. Exactly."

"Keep in mind, though," Luke said, "everyone has a dark side they never show the world. A lot of people have a hidden pain that can sometimes overwhelm them and no one in their lives ever suspects."

Silence fell between them for a moment.

"I know about hidden pain," Sophie finally said, her tone subdued. "But that doesn't mean it always leads to suicide."

"I agree. But sometimes it does—or at least thoughts of it." His low words had her looking at him more closely.

She had a feeling he was speaking from experience. "Did someone you know commit suicide?"

He blinked. "No, nothing like that. I've just worked with a lot of people over the years and I've worked a few suicides. People who've killed themselves, and their families had no idea they were struggling. I guess what I'm saying is that the face a lot of people show the outside world in no way reflects what's really going on inside them."

"Jordan's not like that."

"You know him that well?"

"Yes."

"Huh."

"What does that mean?" she asked.

"I guess I'm just surprised. We've known each other for two years, worked together on a daily basis, and I don't know you like that."

She gaped. "You've never made the effort. Every time you've come into the office, you're like, 'Hi, how are you?' And that's about the extent of it."

He shut his lips and she wondered if she'd spoken out of turn. Asking him about it would have to wait. Luke pulled into the entrance of the park. "Keep going," she said. "You know where the bike trail is, right?"

"Yes."

"I had to come out here on one of Jordan's afternoons off to get his signature on some papers he'd been waiting on. He was running the trail with Snapper and said he'd come in to the office. It was a gorgeous day so I didn't mind getting outside. If it had been raining, I'm not sure I would have offered." She shot him a quick smile.

"Yes, you would have." At her raised brow, he shrugged. "I'm beginning to get to know you a bit, I think."

"It doesn't take long. I'm pretty much an open book."

"Hmm. Somehow, I wonder." He cleared his throat. "Did Jordan have a favorite area out here?"

"Just the Parkway. Sometimes he ran, sometimes he biked, but he always had Snapper with him. And while it's not near here, he also liked to run along the East River."

"Someone else will check there." Luke followed her directions to the entrance. While he drove, she took in the vast landscape unfolding before them. Right in the middle of Queens, the wooded area stretched endlessly. "I don't know, Luke, this place is huge. There's just too much ground to cover."

"That's why so many cops are looking for him."

Already there were a multitude of law enforcement vehicles in the area. No one questioned one more pulling in. Luke got on the radio and reported his position and requested an update. "No one's spotted Jordan yet," he said.

"It's still early." She climbed out of the SUV and waited for Luke to release Bruno and join her. "This doesn't feel right."

"What do you mean?"

"While I know and understand that we're following protocol in the way we're conducting the search, I just feel like we're on the wrong track and wasting precious time. We need to check that letter for fingerprints. Ones that don't match ours."

"It's in an evidence bag. I'll get someone to send it over to the lab immediately. Regardless of where Jordan is, that guy kidnapped you and we need to find out who he is."

"No kidding." She bit her lip and glanced around.

"Jordan likes this path a lot," she said. "Katie says when he needs to be alone, he spends as much time as possible walking, running or biking this trail and praying. She says it calms him and gives him focus."

Officers talked with those enjoying the warm spring day. One held up his phone and showed a young couple the screen. Jordan's picture, no doubt. They both shook their heads and the officer's shoulders slumped slightly, but he nodded and made his way to the next person.

"What is it?" Luke asked her.

"What do you mean?"

"Something's been bothering you—other than the obvious—since we found the letter," Luke said. "So, what is it?"

Sophie pressed her lips together, then looked at him. "The handwriting on the letter was Jordan's."

He stilled. "Are you sure?"

"Of course I'm sure. I see it every day. He's forever writing notes and placing them on my desk."

Luke stared at her. "Why didn't you say something earlier?"

"Because I thought we'd have answers by now. I thought we would have found Jordan and he would have explained everything. The fact that we haven't found him yet scares me to death, because while I don't believe he's suicidal, I definitely believe he's in some kind of serious trouble and time may be running out for him."

* * *

The problem was, Luke mostly agreed with her, although he couldn't deny the little niggling of doubt that wanted to raise its head and demand attention.

He shoved it aside for the moment, slightly ashamed at the flare of uncertainty—and, if he was honest—jealousy of her unwavering loyalty to her boss. It hadn't taken him long to discover there was a depth to Sophie he wouldn't have guessed she possessed.

However, just in the last few hours, she'd proven herself a loyal employee—the kind who worked hard because of her innate integrity, not just because she was earning a paycheck. And she was Jordan's friend as well as his assistant. She would defend those she cared about to the bitter end—including her fierce belief that Jordan wouldn't kill himself. She'd made that abundantly clear.

And yet, Luke hesitated. While he admired that about Sophie, sometimes loyalty and devotion could blind a person to reality. Sometimes. He wasn't saying that was the case with Sophie and their boss, but he wasn't ruling it out either. And a small part of him couldn't help wondering what it would be like to have someone like Sophie in his corner. For someone to have that kind of unshakable devotion to him.

Bruno jerked at the end of the leash, anxious to do his job. Only Luke didn't have a job for him to do. Bruno was a cadaver K-9, whose specialty was finding dead bodies, and Jordan wasn't dead. Luke's jaw tightened, but he followed after the animal, determined to do his part in locating his boss. He had to keep believing it wasn't too late. That *he* wasn't too late. *Please, God, please let us find him—alive—and let there be a reasonable explanation for his disappearance.*

For the next two hours, he and the other officers searched the area without success. Jordan wasn't there. Or at any of his favorite places according to reports coming in.

"Where could he be?" Sophie finally asked on the verge of tears.

Luke's heart slammed against his chest in empathy with her worry. "I don't know. Maybe you're right, though. Maybe we need to sit down with Katie and talk through everything."

"Like what?"

"Like Jordan's morning. His schedule. What he said to her before he left? Everything. There's no detail too small, but I'm pretty confident about one thing."

"What's that?" Sophie asked.

"Jordan never made it to the Parkway this morning."

"Why?"

"Because Bruno didn't even get a hint of his scent. That means he wasn't there."

"Then let's go." Sophie hurried to the SUV and

Luke climbed behind the wheel after making sure Bruno was settled. He paused.

Sophie frowned. "What are you waiting for?"

"Do you have Katie's number?"

"Of course."

"Can you call her? I think we can do this over the phone and it will be faster than going back to the auditorium."

"Sure. I can put her on speaker."

Sophie dialed the number. It only made it through half a ring before Katie answered. "Sophie? Did you find him?"

"No, I'm sorry."

Katie's muffled sob echoed through the phone's speaker, and Luke winced. Katie was one of the sweetest people on the planet and he hated that she was suffering—that they were *all* suffering. "I'm here, too, Katie," Luke said. "Listen, we're not giving up, so just keep hanging in there, okay? But we think you can help."

"Yes. Of course." She sniffed. "Anything. What can I do?"

"Tell me about this morning when you last saw Jordan. What was his mind-set like?"

"Um…nothing unusual. He seemed fine. And by fine, he was joking around about some things, talking about where we'd take our next vacation. He was proud of the graduating K-9s and handlers and said what a great addition they would be to the force. He was looking forward to the future," she said softly. "That note wasn't from him."

"I don't think it was either," Sophie said, "but did you look at it?"

"No, I didn't want to. Why?"

"It was his handwriting."

Katie paused. "Then someone forced him to do it," she said, her voice low, but firm. "The only way he would write that note is if someone held a gun to his head." She paused. "Or threatened me."

"I'd agree with that last part," Sophie said.

"What time did Jordan leave this morning?" Luke asked.

"Before I did—around 8:30. He took Snapper with him for their run, then was supposed to go straight to headquarters, where he was going to use the shower, dress, then head to the auditorium to go over his remarks before the ceremony."

Luke paused, lips pursed. "Did you see him actually get in the vehicle and drive away?"

She paused. "Um…no. I didn't."

"I've got an idea," he said.

"What's that?"

"I don't think Jordan ever made it to the park to take Vanderbilt Parkway. I'm going to get Finn to bring Abernathy to your house and see if the dog can pick up Jordan's scent and at least tell us which way he went when he left the house—and whether or not he was on foot or in his vehicle."

"But the SUV is gone."

"I know." That didn't necessarily mean Jordan was driving it. He kept that to himself. "I'll meet you there."

Luke hung up and dialed Finn's number.

"You find him?" the K-9 officer answered.

"No. Sophie thinks we're going about this all wrong and I have to say I kind of agree with her."

"What do you have in mind?"

"Meet me at Jordan's house with Abernathy. Katie's going to give us one of the chief's shirts and you're going to see how far Abernathy can take you."

"Not a bad idea. I'll meet you there in twenty."

"On the way."

When Luke neared the Jameson home in Rego Park, all he could do was pray Abernathy and Finn would find something that would give the next step in their search for Jordan. The three-story multifamily building was home to the entire Jameson clan.

"We'll need to talk to Alexander and Ivy," Luke said.

Alexander and Ivy Jameson, parents to Noah, Carter, Zach and Jordan, lived on the first floor. Jordan and Katie shared the second floor, and the other brothers, along with Carter's six-year-old daughter, Ellie, had the large third-floor apartment in true *Full House* fashion. Luke knew Carter's wife, Ellie's mother, had died in childbirth, leaving Carter devastated and in need of help with the newborn. The family hadn't hesitated, jumping right in to do whatever Carter needed.

Luke had often envied the tight-knit family that was so very different from his own. With one brother and a father who blamed him for his mother's death, Luke kept his distance from them.

"Mr. and Mrs. Jameson are out of town this week visiting relatives in Florida," Sophie said. "I sure hope we can find Jordan and not have to tell them anything about all of this."

"Okay. Then that's the plan for now."

He parked on the street just as Finn and Abernathy arrived. Katie's car was already in the driveway. The door opened, and she stepped onto the porch. Luke drew in a deep breath. "All right, let's do this."

THREE

Sophie had prayed the entire drive to the Jameson home. Prayed and kept an eye on her phone. Of course it hadn't rung and no one had called in on the radio to report they'd found Jordan. She climbed out of the SUV and stood beside it while Katie approached Finn, holding a bag in her gloved hands.

"Jordy dropped this shirt on the bathroom floor yesterday when he came in from his run," Katie said. "I'm a little embarrassed to say that I left it there simply to see how long it would take him to pick it up. It was a private joke. He leaves his clothes on the floor, I leave my towels." She sniffed and swiped a stray tear, then waved a hand. "Never mind. I'm chattering. I used gloves to put it in the bag so it wouldn't have my scent on it."

Abernathy, the eager-to-work yellow Lab, stood at Finn's side, tail wagging, ears perked, eyes on the bag. The dog's nose quivered as Finn took the bag. "That was good thinking. Are you sure you aren't part cop?"

Katie offered him a small smile. "Being married to Jordy has taught me a lot," she said softly. Tears stood in her eyes. "Please, just find him. I'll never fuss about him leaving his clothes on the floor again."

"That's the plan. Let's start inside."

Sophie and Luke followed Katie, Finn and Abernathy inside. Finn pulled on a glove, then opened the bag and removed the shirt. He held it out to Abernathy, who shoved his nose in it, over it and around it.

Once he was sure the dog had the scent, Finn let him take the lead even though they knew Jordan wasn't inside. There was always the hope Abernathy would lead them to some sort of clue.

Sophie frowned. It was such a long shot. Were they wasting valuable time searching the house when Jordan could be somewhere needing help? But these guys were the best. They did this on a daily basis and would be hyper diligent now that one of their own was missing. She knew this. She could trust them. Sophie kept her lips shut and let the professionals work.

Finally, Abernathy led them to the back door and out into the backyard. K-9 handlers were required to have an outdoor space for their dogs, and this house couldn't be more perfect. Sophie remembered overhearing a conversation about how Alexander and Ivy bought the multifamily house when their sons were little and rented out the other apartments before giving them to their children when they were ready to live on their own. Even while her mind spun with facts she knew, she kept an eye on Abernathy and Finn.

Finn once again let the dog lead, all of his attention tuned to the canine's body language. Abernathy covered the back area, then returned to Finn and sat.

"Nothing back here," Finn said. "Let's try outside the fence." The gate opened into the small driveway that ran the length of the house.

The dog led them out into the street and ran a short distance before stopping and looking back at Finn. Sophie and Luke caught up.

"He's lost the scent," Finn said, "but I think this means that Jordan and Snapper definitely got in the vehicle and took off."

"Then where's the car, and where's Snapper?" Sophie asked.

Luke shook his head. "Jordan could park that K-9 SUV anywhere and no one would think anything about it other than there was a cop somewhere close by. At least not for a while. We've got a BOLO out on it, but people will have to be paying close attention to the license plate."

"I don't know," Sophie said. "Seems to me that might make it even easier to find."

"Always looking for that silver lining, aren't you?"

"Keeping hopeful, Luke, that's all."

"Good," Finn said. "We need to stay hopeful. Prayers wouldn't hurt either."

"What about security footage?" Luke asked. "Katie probably knows the route Jordan takes every morning. We could check any cameras along that drive."

"Good idea. As soon as we get that route, I'll call it in."

"I know the route," Sophie said. She rattled it off.

Finn popped his phone from the clip on his belt. "I'll call it in and we'll see what Dani can pull," he said.

While Finn put in the request, Sophie paced. "The longer, he's missing, the chances of finding him drop," she muttered. They knew that as well as she did. But she wasn't really talking to them, just stating a fact and reminding herself that they needed to find him fast. "So, we know he got up, and his plan was to go for a run with Snapper and then go to headquarters to shower and change. On his way to the auditorium, he might have planned to stop somewhere and grab something quick like toast or a bagel."

"That sounds right," Katie said. "Only he never made it to the auditorium."

Actually, they weren't sure he even made it out of the neighborhood.

They all fell silent until Luke rubbed a hand down his cheek. "There's nothing more we can do here," Luke said. "Let's get back to headquarters. Sophie, would you be willing to go through Jordan's office and see if anything strikes you as off?"

"Of course." Sophie looked at Zach, Katie, Noah and Carter. "Do we need to call your parents?"

Noah shook his head. "No, not yet. It's only been a few hours. I'm not ready to sound the alarm yet."

"Katie," Sophie said, "do you want me to come back and stay here with you after I've gone through his office?"

"No. I'll come back to headquarters." Katie rubbed her arms as though chilled. "I can't stay here right now."

"Are you sure?" Sophie stepped forward and pulled the woman out of earshot of the others. "This is super stressful, and you need to rest. Take care of yourself."

"I know. And I will. But I can't…stay here and do nothing."

Sophie understood that. "All right. You can rest on the sofa in Jordan's office if you need to."

"If I need to. I just want to be where everyone else is, so I can know the updates as they come in."

Katie insisted on driving her own vehicle. Sophie didn't blame her but was worried for her friend. Her pregnant friend whose husband was missing. Sophie ran places and people through her mind, desperately searching for someone who might have a clue where Jordan would be.

"Sophie?" Luke asked "You okay?"

Sophie blinked. And realized she'd been lost in thought the entire ride back to headquarters. She drew in a deep breath. "Yes, sorry. I was just... thinking."

"Are you in pain?"

"My head hurts and my leg is bruised, but time and some ibuprofen will take care of those issues. I can ignore the discomfort for now."

"If you're sure."

"I'm sure." With Sophie favoring her bruised leg, they hurried toward the headquarters building. Just inside, her phone rang. She grabbed it from her pocket and checked the screen, then shook her head at Luke. It wasn't Jordan. His shoulders dropped. "It's my dad," she said, lifting the device to her ear. "Hi, Dad."

"Hey, sweetheart, something kind of weird just happened and I wanted to give you a heads-up."

"Okay. What's going on?"

Luke raised a brow and she shrugged.

"Someone just called here looking for you."

"Looking for me? Who?"

"He said he was a friend from college, that he'd tried calling your number, but when you didn't answer, called me. Then he started asking a lot of personal questions, which I declined to answer, of course. He finally cursed and hung up on me. It's got me worried about you."

Dread curled in the pit of her stomach, adding to the ball of worry for Jordan that was already there. "Okay, thanks for letting me know. I'll take care of it."

"Do you know who it could be?"

"I have an idea." Her gaze locked on Luke's. He stood there listening unabashedly. Sophie didn't care. If she'd wanted privacy, she would have walked into the conference room.

"I have to leave to head for work. It's just an overnight run, but it'll be late tomorrow night before I'm back. You sure it's okay for me to leave?"

A truck driver, he was often gone overnight. As a child, Sophie had wished he could be home more. At this moment, she was glad he was getting out of the city. "I'm sure. I'll talk to you later, Dad. Thanks for letting me know."

"I'm not going to kid you, Sophie, this scares me."

"I know. And I promise I'll take care of it." She paused. "And if I have trouble doing that, I know people who can help."

Her father let out a low laugh. "Yeah, I guess you do. Be careful, hon."

"Always. Have a good trip."

She hung up and stood silent for a moment while she processed.

"What was that all about?" Luke asked.

"My dad is a long-haul trucker and was getting ready to walk out the door for an overnight run when his phone rang." She told him about the call. "I think it's probably the guy who tried to kidnap me this morning digging for information." She shuddered. "What worries me is that he knows my dad's home telephone number. And in order to find that out, he had to know my name—and my dad's."

Luke definitely didn't like the sound of that. He shook his head. "I don't think you should go home. If he knows your name and number—and your father's—he most likely knows your address, too."

"Of course he does. I share a house with my dad and brother. But how would he find that out?" Sophie ran a shaky hand over her bun, then straightened it.

"He knows you work for the K-9 unit here in Queens. He may have even been in the auditorium watching you set up, just waiting for a chance to make his move."

Sophie shuddered. "I did have an eerie sensation of someone watching me. Like someone else was there but didn't want me to know it." She paused and frowned. "As I told you, I even heard something but didn't think much of it."

"It wouldn't be too hard to figure out who was taken from the auditorium. All he had to do was ask someone."

"Oh. Right. I should have thought of that." She fell silent. "Then that means I definitely can't go home. I have a separate apartment from my brother and father, but it's still the same house." A sigh escaped her. "I mean, I have no choice. It's not like I can afford a hotel."

"I have a better idea," Luke said.

"What?"

"Would you be willing to stay at my place?"

"Oh." She chewed her lip.

"Well?"

"I'm thinking."

"There's really nothing to think about."

"What do you mean?"

"I mean, I don't think you're safe and I'd like you to come home with Bruno and me until we can find the guy who kidnapped you." She blinked at him as though having trouble processing his words. "Sophie?" He gave her a slight shake, eyes narrowed with concern. "Are you listening?" Had she gone into some kind of shock? A mental overload?

She finally blinked and met his gaze. "I think I've had enough for today."

"I agree. I'll take you to your place and you can pack a bag. Then we'll go back to my house."

"I think that would really inconvenience you. Don't you have a couple of roommates?"

"Two. Sam and David. The good thing is Sam's out of the country for a couple of days so you can use his room."

The fact that she simply nodded told him how worn-out she was—and was probably hurting even though she hadn't said a word about being in pain. "How does some ibuprofen sound?"

"Like a really good idea."

"You better keep some in your system. You're going to feel it tomorrow even more."

"I know. Thanks."

Luke led the way to his Tahoe and Bruno jumped into his spot in the back. Sophie settled into the passenger seat and buckled up. Bruno leaned forward and settled his snout on her left shoulder, then licked her cheek with a swipe of his long tongue.

Luke gaped. "Bruno!"

"Don't fuss at him," Sophie said, wiping her cheek on her shoulder. "It's sweet. I think he knows I need comforting and is offering it." She scratched the dog's ears, and Bruno rolled his eyes to Luke as though gloating in his successful attempt to gain Sophie's attention.

Luke scowled at the animal, but it didn't seem to faze the dog. With a huff, Luke pulled from the parking lot and headed for Sophie's home in Woodside.

It didn't take long to reach it and he turned onto her street. "Nice house," he said.

"I like it. It's been in the family forever. My brother and father live upstairs, and I have the downstairs. Someday, I hope to afford something of my own but for now, this works for me." She quirked a small smile at him. The first one he'd seen all day. Then she scratched Bruno under his chin. Again. "I'd like a dog," she said, "but dogs need space to run. I have a yard, but it's too small for the size dog I'd want."

"That's why K-9 officers are required to have a yard." He smiled. She knew that, of course, but it was small talk. Something to keep her mind on anything but the events of the day—and his off the fact that he was jealous of his dog.

He cleared his throat. "You ready?"

"Sure."

He and Bruno followed Sophie to the front door of her duplex-style home.

Which was cracked open.

She gasped and stepped back.

"That's not supposed to be open, I'm guessing?" Luke whispered.

"No."

"Stand back against the wall next to the door.

Bruno, stay." In the blink of an eye, the dog's de-meanor changed at Luke's command. His ears went up and he was in instant work mode, waiting for the next order. Bruno sat next to Sophie and she placed a hand on his head. Luke pulled his weapon and stood to the side of the door. Using his left hand, he gave the metal door a light shove. It swung inward on well-oiled hinges.

Luke stepped over the threshold and glanced to the right. Kitchen with the stove light on. Living area to the left. Hallway straight ahead with the bathroom at the end and the bedroom to the left. Small and efficient.

And trashed. Sofa cushions lay on the floor along with the lamps that had probably been on the end tables. The intruder hadn't spared the small buffet in the eating area either and the draw-ers had been yanked out, dishes crushed onto the hardwood floor.

A loud crash came from the bedroom area and Luke headed down the hallway. "NYPD! Come out of the room, hands where I can see them! Now!"

Silence.

"I'm not playing!" Luke said. "Come out with your hands where I can see them!"

A black-clad figure shot out of the room and slammed into Luke hard enough to knock the breath from him. And his gun from his grip. The weapon hit the floor and skittered across the wood out of reach. Gasping, Luke threw a blind punch that grazed a whiskered jaw.

Bruno growled and lunged forward, snapping at the attacker, who stumbled back, tripped and fell with a thud to the wood floor. Only to lurch to his feet and come forward swinging as Bruno moved in. He caught the dog on the ear. Bruno yelped and darted away, shaking his head.

Luke dove after the man and wrapped a hand around an ankle, yanking him back to the floor. Bruno added his displeasure and snapped his teeth in the man's face.

A foot kicked out and landed a hard blow to Luke's temple, stunning him. Stars spun in front of his eyes.

Again, the assailant managed to find his feet—and headed for Sophie. She darted away. Bruno barked and launched himself at the man once more, this time closing his teeth around an arm. The pained scream echoed through the apartment.

Luke rolled in time to see Sophie swing a lamp into the man's chest. The lamp fell, hitting Bruno's snout before crashing to the floor. The dog flinched and released the attacker, who rushed out the door.

Then Bruno was beside Luke, nudging him and whining.

Luke shook his head. While everything had happened in mere seconds, Luke raged that he couldn't move fast enough. Finally, he made it to his feet while his head spun and nausea curled in his gut. "Sophie!"

"I'm okay." She rushed to him. "Are you?"

"Fine. I've just got to learn to duck." He grabbed his weapon and raced to the front door in time to see the man hop into a light gray Jeep he'd had double-parked four doors down and peel away from the building. Luke slapped a hand against his thigh. He couldn't see the license plate.

He snagged his phone and called it in with what little information he had. When he hung up, he drew in a deep breath and pressed a hand to his aching head, then turned to Sophie, who now sat on the sofa with Bruno's big head resting on her knee. She examined the animal's ear and nose with gentle fingers.

"Is he okay?" Luke asked. "Do I need to get him to the vet?"

"I think he was just stunned, but if you would feel better taking him to the vet, we can do that."

Luke looked his partner over and sighed with relief when he found nothing concerning. "Good boy, Bruno." The dog licked his hand, then turned back to Sophie and nudged her hand.

With the danger past, Luke allowed himself to take a moment to simply watch her. She continued to scratch Bruno's ears, and Luke was hit with the longing to take the dog's place. A brief flash of the two of them sitting on the couch, watching a movie and sharing a bowl of popcorn held him frozen for a second.

"Luke?" she asked. "You okay?"

He blinked. "Yeah, fine. Officers are on the way."

"I'm sorry."

"About what?" He stilled and frowned.

"For not finding a weapon or some way to help you."

Luke went to her and pulled her into a hug. "It's okay. I was just worried about you." And because the feel of her in his arms made his head spin way too much, he released her and stepped back.

"I'm going to call my dad," she said. "I need to let him know what happened. And I need to call Trey."

"Of course."

She dialed her brother's number, waited, then hung up. "He's not answering."

"Try your dad."

She did, and Luke couldn't help notice her sigh of relief when he answered on the first ring. "Hey, Dad, I know you're on the road, but I need to let you know someone broke into my place." Pause. "No, I'm fine. I'm with a friend from the station. Do you know where Trey is?" She shook her head at Luke. "Trey went hiking with friends and won't be back until Saturday," she said, then went back to the phone and explained the fact that she was going to stay with Luke and his roommates for a while.

Her father said something, and she nodded with a glance at Luke. "I'm sure, Dad. I'll be safe there and, hopefully, whoever broke in won't be back. You still have several dinners in the freezer for when you get back from your run and most of the clothes are washed. Hopefully, by the time you and Trey get back, all of this will be over."

Luke watched her, considering her words and what they meant.

She hung up and caught his gaze. "What? Why are you looking at me like that?"

"You do a lot for them, don't you?"

She shrugged. "My dad's done a lot for me." She paused. "Don't you help your family out when they need it?"

"Not really. We don't talk much."

"Oh. That's...sad."

"I know." He cleared his throat. "But forget about that. While I want to hear more about your family, why don't you start taking inventory? Just don't touch anything. When the officers get here, they'll take prints. Ours are on file so they'll be able to eliminate those."

She shook her head as her gaze swept the area. "I don't think he took anything. He just broke everything."

Luke noticed the shattered flat screen television

on the floor. Her iPad and Blu-ray player lay in front of the television stand. Also broken.

"He stomped on them," she whispered. "Why?" Tears leaked from her eyes and she swiped them away with an angry brush of her fingers. Before Luke could answer or offer more comfort, she leaned over and picked up a figurine from the floor. "This was on my coffee table. He swept it to the floor, but it didn't break, which is a relief. A friend gave it to me." She paused, studying it. "Although, it's worth several hundred dollars. And yet, he left it."

"Which means he was probably looking for something and this wasn't a random criminal simply after items to sell for easy money."

She frowned. "But what?"

He nodded to the corner of the room. "Your desk is turned upside down. If this was the same guy who called your father looking for you, then maybe he was searching for something that would tell him how to find you. And when he couldn't, he took his frustration out on your stuff."

"Why didn't he just wait until I got home?" A pause. "Then again, maybe he did. Maybe he was in my bedroom just waiting to…" She shuddered. "I'm so glad you were here."

Luke's heart twisted. He went to her again and wrapped his arms around her to pull her into a hug once more. He could put his own feelings on hold and simply offer her comfort. For a moment, she stiffened, then leaned against him.

"I'm sorry, Sophie," he said softly. "I know this has been a rotten day for you."

"It's been even more rotten for Katie," she mumbled.

"Yeah. I can't argue with that." He sighed. And realized he didn't want to let her go. While he could tell she was finding comfort in the embrace, he realized he was, too. Which made him frown. While she was changing his perception of her, he reminded himself she was still young. Very young.

Bruno nosed in between them and Sophie let out a watery laugh.

"I think he's feeling left out." She scratched his neck and the dog sighed his contentment. "All's right with his world, isn't it? He's just happy to be with those he loves and having his ears scratched."

"Yes, he's pretty easy to please. Ear scratches, belly rubs and a hug every once in a while."

"I think everyone could learn a few lessons from this guy," she said softly.

"Amen to that."

"Did you know we're getting a new dog?"

"Who? You and your family?"

She laughed. "No, the department. Her name's Stella and she's a gift from the Czech Republic. She's supposed to be really special." Bruno licked her cheek and she huffed another choked laugh. "But not as special as you, Bruno, I promise."

Luke's phone buzzed, and he snatched it to check the screen.

"Who is it?" Sophie asked.

"A group text from Katie. Just wanting an update."

"Oh."

While all was right with Bruno's world, Luke's was standing on its head. And Katie was growing more and more desperate as time passed without hearing from her husband. Frankly, he couldn't blame her. Luke closed his eyes and hugged Sophie once again, this time allowing himself to take comfort from her. He said a silent prayer that Katie would get to hold Jordan in the near future.

Please let us find him.

FOUR

Sophie decided she could stay right there in Luke's arms for the rest of eternity. However, that wouldn't be very productive when it came to finding Jordan. And not only that, she had no business letting her attraction for the man influence her into letting a romance develop. But she had her brother and her father to look after. Romance wasn't in the near future for her.

Before the thought could depress her, a knock on the door had her slipping from his embrace. "I guess I should pack a bag after they process this place, huh?"

"I think that would be a good idea."

Luke let the two officers inside and made the introductions. Sophie forced a smile. "Thank you for coming so quickly."

"Of course," the one nearest her said. "We're just going to do our thing."

"Perfect," Sophie said.

It didn't take long for them to finish. Once

they were gone, she forced herself to face the destruction in her bedroom. Slashed pillows spilled their filling and her blinds had been ripped from the windows. Drawers had been overturned and the contents littered the floor next to the dresser. What bothered her the most was the fact that her bedside lamp had been thrown against her mirror, shattering both items. What reason could he have had for such wanton destruction in here?

It was almost like the person was mad at her and wanted her to know it. He'd made the whole break-in personal. Which probably meant that he hadn't gotten what he'd come for.

Her.

With a shudder, she ignored the mess and pulled three outfits for work from her closet, some jeans and T-shirts and anything else she thought she might need. Next, she added toiletries from the bathroom. Thankfully, it didn't look like he'd touched that room.

Rolling her small suitcase behind her, she walked back into the living area where Luke and Bruno waited. "I think I've got everything I'll need for a few days. With access to a laundromat, I can even stretch that."

"Good," Luke said. He led the way back to his vehicle, Bruno trotting along beside him. Once Sophie was buckled and Bruno was settled in his area, she drew in a deep breath and closed her eyes for a brief moment.

"How are you holding up?" Luke asked.

"My head is pounding, and every muscle feels like it's been through a rigorous workout, but I'm alive and I'm grateful. What about you? How's your head?"

"Pounding a bit like yours, I imagine, but I'll be okay."

When his right hand curled around her left, Sophie took comfort once again from his touch. "Thank you for staying with me," she said softly. "I can't tell you how much I appreciate it. I don't know what I'd do if I had to face all of this alone."

"Of course." With a gentle squeeze of her fingers, he released her hand and turned the key. The Tahoe purred to life and Luke headed toward his apartment.

"Are you sure this is going to be okay?" she asked. "I really don't want to put you out or cause any inconvenience."

"I'm positive it's all right. Like I said, Sam is out of the country on business and David is working the late shift. He'll be home around midnight."

"Tell me what they do again?"

"Sam's a consultant for a software company. David is a fireman. He works out of the station near our home."

"You like them. I can hear it in your voice."

"I do. They're great guys—and even fun to hang out with occasionally in spite of the fact that they're not cops." He quirked a smile and slid a glance at her. She bit her lip, still concerned she might be in the way. "Don't worry," he said. "We don't live in a pigsty or anything. The place is almost ridiculously neat."

"That hadn't even crossed my mind, but why do I sense a story behind that?"

"Sam's mother has adopted David and me. She comes by twice a week to clean and drop off food."

"Wow."

"Yeah, no kidding. But we don't mind. Sam's father passed away about six months ago, so we let his mom do what she wants. It keeps her busy and helps us out at the same time."

"I'd say that's a wonderful arrangement for everyone involved."

A short time later, he parked in a free spot and they walked down the block to a three-family house. The houses were packed together along the narrow street. He had told her that he and his roommates rented the apartment on the first floor.

Sophie hadn't been to his home before and she couldn't help admiring the small, well-kept front area around the steps leading up to the door. She spotted roses and daffodils and a few other colorful bulbs she couldn't identify. "The flowers are beautiful. Really gorgeous. Who's the green thumb?"

"Thanks. All three of us enjoy the work when we have a day off. It's kind of a stress reliever."

Stress reliever. She could use one of those. Tears flooded her eyes, the surge of emotion taking her by surprise.

"Sophie?"

"I can't believe this is happening," she whispered. "Where can Jordy be, Luke?"

With a heavy sigh, he shook his head. "I don't know, but we'll find him." A pause. "You call him Jordy?"

She shrugged and shoved the tears away. "He said it was okay one afternoon when I was eating with him and Katie. She called him Jordy and told me I'd graduated to that of trusted friend and had the honor of using his family name." Her gaze met his. "It's been too long. Too many hours are passing with no word. You know as well as I the longer we go without hearing from him, the more likely it is we—" She bit her lip.

"Won't," he finished for her. "I know. I'm worried, too, but we won't give up. Hopefully, Jordan will call before too long and we can all get back to business as usual."

"Yeah." She slipped out of the seat and followed him up the steps and inside to the shared foyer.

The wood floors gleamed. He led her to the far end of the short hallway and opened the door to his apartment. Once inside, she looked around. It sparkled. "Wow, you weren't kidding. It's super clean."

"Yep. And since Sam's mom was here this

morning, his room should be nice and shiny, too. Clean sheets, clean towels, the works. He has a bathroom attached so you'll have all the privacy you need."

He pulled her suitcase behind him and she soon found herself in a bright, if masculine, bedroom. "It's lovely," she said, forcing a smile to her lips. She loved the room. She hated the reason she was using it.

"I'll just leave you to get settled while I go inspect the refrigerator," he said. "Are you hungry?"

"Starving."

"Give me a few minutes and we'll eat."

Fifteen minutes later, dressed in yoga pants and a long sweatshirt, she padded into the kitchen, where she found Luke dishing up something that smelled delicious. "Chicken cordon bleu?"

"I think so. Sometimes I'm not sure what she brings, but it's always good."

"Do you eat like this every night?"

He flushed. "Well, not *every* night."

"You guys are spoiled completely rotten. I feel sorry for your future wives. If you even *want* to get married."

"Hey, now, what's that supposed to mean?"

She giggled at his affront. "Well, really, take a look around. You have a spotless apartment, gourmet food at the push of a button and no one to nag you about taking the trash out. Why would you need to get married?"

His eyes locked on hers. "Maybe I wouldn't mind too much about being nagged to take out the trash."

Her breath caught somewhere between her lungs and her throat. "Oh. Well. Okay, then."

A slight smile tilted the corners of his lips, then he frowned. A sad one. "But I don't know that it'll ever happen for me."

"Why not?" Frankly, she would have thought he'd have plenty of opportunities to find himself engaged and married. A twinge of jealousy flashed, and she shoved it away.

He shook his head. "I'm not really marriage material. At least that's what I've been told."

She blinked. "Who told you that?"

"An ex-girlfriend." His lips tightened, then relaxed as though he'd forced it. "What about you? You have any plans for marriage in the future?"

"In the future, maybe. Not necessarily the *near* future, but yes, I think I'd like to get married. One day. To the right person, of course."

"Of course. So, you haven't met Mr. Right yet?"

Sophie laughed. "I don't know. There's no one on my radar right now." Except…she had a feeling if she looked close at that radar, she might see Luke right there—a little blip on her screen. As a potential boyfriend. Should she be looking. Which she wasn't. Her father and brother needed her. Well, her father did anyway. Being married or even dating would severely cut into the time that she would have to be there for her dad. The thought hadn't bothered her much before. But now, looking at Luke, she had to admit, she almost wished things could be different. But she couldn't help wondering... "What was it that made you 'not marriage material'?"

His jaw tightened. "Ah, well, according to the ex, I'm too serious, need to loosen up and learn how to have a good time." He grimaced. "And I work too much. She let me know in no uncertain terms that I would never be Mr. Right for her."

"She sounds terribly immature. I'm glad you got out of that relationship."

"I am, too." He studied her with a look that sent heat surging into her cheeks. She cleared her throat and shrugged. Then winced when the action tugged at sore muscles. She used her opposite hand to massage the area. "I sure met Mr. Wrong today." A shudder shook her.

"I'll say. But you have time. You're young."

"And what are you?" She lifted a brow, shaking off the remembered terror. "A stodgy old bachelor?"

A light snort escaped him, and he offered another grin, but she thought she saw something different in his gaze. Something...interesting and worth exploring.

"That's me. Old and set in my ways."

But he might be willing to change some of those ways. For Sophie anyway. Right now, Luke found himself wishing he wasn't quite so old. Not that thirty-three was ancient, but the nine-year age difference made him grimace. And what was up with him blurting out that he wasn't marriage material anyway? He might think that, but he didn't need to pass that on to her. She'd thrown up a few walls as soon as the words had passed his lips. One thing she was right about, though, was the more time that passed without finding Jordan, the more his nerves tightened.

"How about a change of subject while we eat?" he asked.

"Sure." She took a bite of the chicken and closed her eyes. "This is wonderful."

He waited for her to look at him before nodding. "I can't stop thinking about Jordan."

"I know. Same here," she said softly. "And Katie. My heart hurts for her."

"Which is why we've got to keep thinking. Can you recall anything that would suggest Jordan has any enemies?"

Sophie set her fork on the table and rubbed her eyes. "No, not right offhand. I mean, he was mostly behind a desk these days, but before he was chief, he worked the streets just like you guys. I'm sure there are some criminals he arrested who still hold a grudge, but there've been no threats, no weird phone calls, *nothing*."

"Unless he just didn't tell you about them."

"True, but I would think I would have noticed *something* if that was going on."

"What about any problems at headquarters? With other officers or anyone else who works there?"

"There are the usual complaints, but nothing we haven't dealt with before and nothing stands out at all. This is so frustrating!"

"I know." Her facial expressions fascinated him. He found himself thinking he could watch her indefinitely. "I admire you, Sophie."

She blinked and some of the ire faded from her eyes. "What makes you say that?"

"I've known you for a couple of years now, right?"

"Yes. I started working at the K-9 unit right out of college, and we met my second day on the job."

She remembered that? "But we've never really gotten to know each other on a personal basis."

"No, just pretty much in passing. Why?"

"Because you're just not what I expected or would have imagined."

She raised a brow. "What does that mean?"

"Don't take this the wrong way, but you're so young and yet so mature." And so attractive. Her youth had kept him from looking at her twice in the past and now he found himself regretting his quick judgment.

"Chalk it up to life experiences," she said.

"I had to grow up pretty fast after my mother walked out."

Whoa. He hadn't been expecting that. "How old were you when she left?"

"I'd just turned ten. One day she was there, the next she wasn't." She shrugged, but he sensed the hurt beneath the gesture.

"I'm so sorry."

"I am, too. For a long time I wondered if it was my fault."

"What? Why?"

"I...wasn't the best or brightest student and my parents fought a lot about me. Later, I was diagnosed with a learning disability and things changed dramatically for me after that, but Mom was already gone." She shook her head. "Anyway, as you can imagine, my dad was thrown for a while. He struggled with depression, but later told me that my brother and I were his world and his reason to keep going. I didn't realize how rough it was on him at the time, but now I look back and can see how hard he worked to be there for us."

"Well, if you're any indication of the type of dad he was, then he must have been pretty amazing."

Her flush made him smile.

"He was super amazing, so thank you," she said softly. "Still is. He's always looking out for me and my brother."

"And you look out for them, don't you?"

"I do. After Mom left, I knew I had to be the one to pick up the pieces." She shrugged. "It was hard, but we managed."

"Do you know where your mom is now?"

"I think she was in Texas the last time I heard. I don't talk to her very often."

"You don't hold a grudge?"

Sophie sighed. "I was angry for a long time. A very long time. But I came to realize that she just wasn't cut out to be a mother and Trey and I were probably better off without her. My grandmother—Dad's mom—stepped in and helped quite a bit when she could, so she was a good influence."

"But not the mom you needed."

"No."

"You became that for Trey, didn't you?"

"How could you tell?"

"Just a hunch."

"I'm five years older than Trey. He was still a baby when she left, and even though I was only ten, I suppose it was only natural that I would mother him. But," she sighed, "he's nineteen now and trying to stretch his wings and figure life out."

"Kids do that."

"I know, but..."

"What?" he asked.

"It's hard to let go."

"Lots of things are hard to let go of, but sometimes it's better for everyone if we can manage to do that."

She went still, her eyes studying him with an intensity that had him working hard not to squirm.

"What is it?" he finally blurted.

"Tell me about her," Sophie said.

"Who?"

"The woman who hurt you so terribly. I know she said you weren't marriage material but tell me more. That's who you were thinking of just now when you talked about letting go, wasn't it?"

Luke flinched. He couldn't help it. "Yes. She was young like you—which is what made me so surprised at your maturity—and she had a crush on me. At least I thought so." He shrugged. "I was new to the K-9 unit and she liked the idea of dating a cop. And I wasn't opposed to dating a pretty woman who had the ability to make me laugh."

"Pretty, huh?"

"She was. But I'm not completely shallow. I genuinely liked her." He shrugged. "Or thought I did."

"But?"

"But she wasn't serious about the relationship. At first that was okay, but then she decided she didn't like all the hours I was putting in. She wanted to go out, have fun, not catch meals during breaks and at odd hours."

"So, you weren't marriage material because you were dedicated to your job and chose to honor the commitment you made instead of blowing it off to make her happy?"

He hesitated then gave a low laugh. "Yes. Exactly."

"I'm sorry, but it sounds to me like she was the one who wasn't marriage material. I didn't exactly have the best role models, but even I know marriage is more than just fun and games. It's teamwork, hard work and it takes commitment. Honestly, she sounds a lot like my mother. You were wise to let her go."

"I know." His jaw tightened at the memories. "But trust me, I won't make that mistake again."

She continued to eye him, curiosity and sympathy coating her gaze. "What was it about her that you fell for?"

He flushed.

"What?" she pressed.

"I had a bit of an ego, and she made me feel like I was someone important. Unfortunately, as time went on, her immaturity was something that I just couldn't deal with—especially when it came to my job. If I had to leave in the middle of dinner or had to cancel a date due to a case, then she would pout for days. We had a pretty big blowup when I called her on her immaturity. She didn't like it."

"I'm sure that was difficult."

"Very." He rubbed a hand over his chin.

"I'm sorry."

"For?"

"For her. For you. For a lot of things." She touched his cheek. "She lost out on a lot, but I'm glad you figured it out before it went any further."

"Yeah. Me, too."

"The experience has made you distrustful," she said softly.

"I don't know if *distrustful* is the right word. *Careful* might be a better description."

"Hmm…"

"What's that mean?"

Sophie shrugged and grimaced. She reached up to rub her shoulder and Luke frowned. "Are you okay?"

"Just sore."

"Here. Let me help." His hand replaced hers and he began a gentle massage of the tight muscles. "Your shoulders are like rocks."

"I know. It's the worry for Jordan, I'm sure."

"That's probably part of it, but the wreck didn't help. Nor the break-in. You're going to really feel this tomorrow."

She glanced up at him with a smile. "I'll survive."

He found himself ensnared in her innocent gaze. When his eyes dropped to her lips and the desire to close the distance hit him, he pulled in a deep breath and stood. "I'd better let you get some sleep."

A flush heated her cheeks and she nodded. "That's a good idea."

"If you hear noises and footsteps, it's just David coming in from his shift."

"Okay."

"Unless you hear me yell and tell you differently."

"Hopefully, that won't happen."

"Hopefully," he echoed. She didn't move, and Luke lifted a hand to touch her cheek. "I haven't talked to anyone like that in a long time," he said. "It was nice."

"I thought so, too."

Her pulse fluttered in her throat and he stepped back. "Good night, Sophie."

"Night, Luke."

She disappeared down the hall and he waited until the door shut with a soft snick before letting out the breath he'd been holding. "Whoa," he said softly to the empty room. "What just happened?"

The silence had no answer for him, but one thing was for sure. It couldn't happen again.

She was too young, too sweet, too innocent. He'd fallen for that before and look where that had gotten him.

No, from now on, he'd keep things strictly professional between them. Certainly no kissing— or even *wanting* to kiss her. *That* had come out of nowhere. And now he couldn't stop thinking about it.

But he had to.

Because he was going to keep things strictly professional.

Because if he didn't, his heart wouldn't survive. And he didn't have time for distractions no matter how pretty she was. He had a boss—and friend— to find. He just prayed he would find him alive.

FIVE

Sophie couldn't help but think about the conversation with Luke from last night even while she hurried to get ready for work. Something had clicked between them and while she wouldn't lie to herself and pretend she wasn't interested in him, she couldn't pursue anything either. Not that he would be welcome to her interest.

He'd already said he wouldn't make the mistake of falling for someone so much younger than him. She almost had to smile at the irony. She'd had to grow up so fast, she never really thought about her age as a number. There'd been some days growing up she'd felt as ancient as dirt.

Her age notwithstanding, she just couldn't get involved with anyone right now. Not when her father and brother needed and counted on her so much. So she could just stop thinking about it—and Luke. Her top priority was finding her boss—and Snapper. Because if she found one, the other had to be close by.

A knock on the door jolted her. "Yes?"

"I heard you moving around," Luke said from the other side. "I thought I'd tell you to dress comfortable. We're taking over the next shift in looking for Jordan. I'll explain more in the car."

"I'll be out in just a few minutes."

"I'll have coffee and a bagel ready. That okay?"

"Perfect."

She found her phone and voice texted Katie. How are you holding up?

Not well. He's never gone this long without contacting me. He's certainly never gone all night. I'm so scared, Sophie. The fact that the reply came so quick said Katie was sitting by her phone.

I know. I am, too. Hang in there, Katie, we'll find him. We have to.

I'm trying hard to believe that and not listen to the little voice that knows all the statistics for missing people. I'm praying. It's all I can do.

I'm adding my prayers to yours. Text or call if you need anything. Even if it's to have a momentary breakdown. I'll listen. And probably join you.

Thank you, Sophie. Just knowing you're out there looking for him helps so much. I can't tell you how much I appreciate that everyone is going all out in trying to find him.

Absolutely. We love him, too.

Sophie tucked her phone away and drew in a steadying breath. She went into the kitchen to find Luke and the young man she assumed to be David, one of his roommates. "Good morning."

"Morning," Luke said. He made the introductions.

Bruno lay stretched on a rug in the corner. He lifted his head and popped to his feet to amble over and give her hand a nudge, silently asking for some attention. She scratched his ears while she inhaled the smell of fresh-brewed coffee. Her mouth watered.

David drained his mug and stood. "Sorry to meet you and run, but I promised to cover part of a shift this morning. Pleasure to have you staying here, though."

"Thank you. You're very kind."

"I'll be home to crash later, though. I hope you find Jordan," he said softly. "I'll be keeping my eyes and ears open, too."

He left, and Luke handed her a to-go cup of coffee and a bagel. "We don't want to be late. So how'd you sleep?" he asked and motioned for Bruno to come. The dog loped over to the door and sat, tail thumping his eagerness to get the day started.

"Pretty well, all things considering," Sophie said.

"Yeah."

"Have you heard anything more about Jordan?"

"That was one of the things I was going to fill you in on. Zach called his parents last night when Jordan didn't turn up. They're on their way home. I think they land sometime within the hour."

"Good, I'm glad they told them. And sad, too, because it means they felt they had to."

"And that's not all."

"Okay." Her gut tightened.

"They found his vehicle," Luke said. He opened the door and a soft breeze blew across her face, letting her know it was going to be a warm day.

"Where?" Katie hadn't said anything in their short text exchange so she must not know. "And when?"

"At the biking trail about five minutes before you walked in the kitchen."

"Wait a minute. They found his car near the biking trail we searched yesterday? At the Vanderbilt Parkway?"

He glanced at his watch and frowned, silently urging her toward the vehicle. "That's right. Officers found it on a routine check of the area. A check they were doing more often in hopes that Jordan would show up. Instead, they found his vehicle."

Sophie planted herself in front of him and he stopped. "That wasn't there yesterday," she said. "We—and other officers—searched every square inch of that bike trail."

"I know. It had to have been left there during the night. Danielle's working on pulling surveillance footage." He continued toward the SUV and Sophie hurried after him and Bruno.

Luke started the SUV and backed out of the short drive. "I don't get it. Why leave the vehicle there?"

"Lots of reasons."

"Like what?"

"I don't know, but there has to be something."

They fell silent, and he drove for the next few minutes while they contemplated why Jordan would leave his vehicle there—but not call in to let anyone know where he was or what he was doing.

Finally, Luke sighed. "I don't know. I can't figure it out." A pause. "You mind answering a couple of questions for me?"

"Of course not."

"What was school like for you?"

She bit her lip and looked away. "That's your question?"

"Is it weird?"

"A bit."

"Humor me. I have a reason for asking."

Sophie hesitated, and he thought she might refuse to answer before she gave a slight shrug.

"School was a nightmare before the diagnosis. Mom and Dad had some knock-down, drag-out fights about my grades and Mom used to yell at me that I wasn't trying and that I was stupid. Dad would yell at her for yelling at me and Trey would just cry."

Luke drew in a harsh breath. "That's awful. I had a feeling it was. Which leads me to my biggest question."

"What?"

"How did you turn out so…?"

"So what?"

"Great. Grounded. Self-confident. I could go on, but you get the idea."

A smile tilted her lips in spite of the memories. "My dad. He was my rock. My brother's, too, although Trey had a harder time of it. I don't think he's ever really dealt with Mom's desertion. He was always a quiet kid, but after Mom left, he really withdrew. It's only lately that he's starting to come into his own." By joining the Marines, though? She still hadn't talked to him about that. And truly, if she thought that's what he really needed to do, she wouldn't fight him on it, but he'd always dreamed of becoming an engineer and she didn't want to see him throw that dream away. Then again, he could always study that while in the service. Maybe she just needed to admit she was having a hard time letting go.

"I'm sorry," Luke said.

What? Oh. "Me, too. But Dad's always been there for us. When I was first diagnosed with the learning disability, I was crushed, but Dad raised me to understand that I'm more than a label. He helped me come to know and believe that I have a purpose in life, that I have choices. And if I make the *right* choices, I can overcome and do pretty much anything I set my mind to."

"I think I'd really like your dad."

"You would. I'll have to introduce you sometime." She snapped her mouth shut. Now, what had made her say that? "I mean, if you—" She needed to zip her lips. He had no interest in meeting her father. Worry for Jordan was making her grasp at anything that might serve as a distraction. Was that where the attraction for Luke was stemming from? As a way to distract herself?

Maybe.

But she didn't think so.

"I'd love to meet your dad sometime, Sophie." His soft response had her swallowing.

So…what did that mean?

Nothing. It meant nothing. He was being polite and kind and doing his best to keep things from being awkward. She appreciated that but reminded herself that she needed to keep her focus and not let Luke distract her.

At least not yet. She still had a brother to put through college and a father to take care of. And she needed to keep her attention on finding Jordan until he was safely home with Katie and all was right with the world again.

Please, God, let us find Jordan.

Luke had to admit he wasn't sure what to think about Sophie anymore. She was smart and beautiful and had thrown his whole mental and emotional well-being into confusion. Generally, he stayed away from the idea of dating anyone who even seemed like they wanted to play head games with him—no matter what age, but especially younger women.

But he had a gut feeling that he wouldn't have to worry about any of that kind of thing with Sophie. He was almost convinced that she didn't know anything about playing head games, and if she did, she was above doing it.

He'd spent two years seeing Sophie on a daily basis. How had he been so blind to her true personality? How had he missed that she apparently had more layers than an onion? Because he'd made a snap judgment effectively limiting his ability to see past the exterior. The more he learned about Sophie, the more he wanted to know.

But right now, he needed to keep his focus. What he wanted most was to find Jordan alive and well with some kind of rational explanation for his disappearing act.

Luke wheeled in to the parking area of the walking trail, dodging one of the park's many landscaping trucks that was being ordered from the area. The man shut the tailgate and climbed into the cab of the truck. With a salute, he vacated the parking lot.

Finn and his dog, Abernathy, along with the Jameson brothers, Noah, Carter and Zach, had gathered in a huddle. Probably discussing the best course of action to take from this point. First thing would be to make sure the vehicle was secured, then decide if the crime scene unit needed to be called. If Jordan had driven the vehicle here himself, then all would end well.

If not, then...

They would fan out and let Finn and Abernathy take the lead searching the area for Jordan. The others had left their dogs in their respective vehicles so as not to be a distraction to Abernathy.

Luke debated about bringing Bruno. For now, he left him in the SUV. He and Sophie approached Noah, who stood next to the abandoned K-9 vehicle. The two officers who'd found it had already taped it off. Just in case. The visible declaration that this was a possible crime scene sent a wave of nausea through Luke.

Please don't let this be for real. The thought blipped through his mind before he could snuff it. There had been a few crime scenes where he'd simply wanted to turn around and leave, call it a bad nightmare and forget about it. Unfortunately, he'd had to work every one of those. Just like he'd work this one. For Jordan.

Sophie stopped outside the perimeter of the yellow tape while Luke ducked under it.

K-9 officer Gavin Sutherland had Tommy, his bomb detection Springer spaniel, sniffing at the back of the SUV. Gavin looked up and Luke raised a brow. The other officer shrugged. "Didn't figure it would hurt to be cautious the way things were playing out. No one believes Jordan killed himself, which means foul play is most likely involved in his disappearance."

Gavin nodded to Sophie. "Someone tried to snatch her because she caught him planting that note in the folder. And now Jordan's vehicle is found in plain sight exactly where Jordan was planning to go, but Jordan's not with it?" He shook his head. "Tommy and I were here. I figured we might as well make sure there aren't any explosives around."

That was so like Gavin and his "better safe than sorry" motto that Luke didn't even blink. "And?"

"We're all good. It's clear." Gavin stepped aside with Tommy. Luke drew in a deep breath and slipped on a pair of gloves. At the driver's side, he opened the door. He'd look for clues about Jordan's possible whereabouts—and determine if the crime scene unit needed to be called.

Finn opened the passenger door and shot him a

frown. "What'd you bring Sophie for? This isn't exactly her beat."

Luke met his friend's gaze. "She was kidnapped yesterday. Then when I took her home, her place was trashed."

Finn's right brow rose. "I knew about the kidnapping, of course. Didn't know about the break-in. That's not a coincidence."

"I don't think so either. I figure she's safer with me than on her own where someone can have another go at her." Luke paused. "Besides, think about it. Other than Katie, Sophie probably spends the most time with Jordan. She handles his business calendar as well as some of his personal stuff. If she can give us information we don't have to bother Katie with, then I'm all for that."

"You've convinced me." Finn drew in a deep breath. "Let's see what we can find."

Together, they searched, looking for anything that would give them information about Jordan. All officers had been trained in forensic evidence handling, so searching the car wouldn't be called into question should a court case result.

Which Luke prayed wouldn't happen. His gut was screaming otherwise and ignoring it was taking a lot of willpower.

A glance over his shoulder sent determination through him. Jordan's solemn brothers stayed back without being asked. They must have come to the same conclusion. Finding Jordan's empty vehicle wasn't good and, as much as they might wish otherwise, had the potential to be very, very bad.

If Jordan was a victim of a crime, they could have no part in the investigation or they would risk the evidence being thrown out should anything come of it. But they would watch and listen and try to help in every other way possible, offering suggestions and advice.

Carter said something, and Noah nodded while Zach frowned then pointed to Jordan's vehicle. Carter and Noah headed for the trail, dogs trotting along beside them while Zach jutted his jaw and kept his eyes trained on the action around the vehicle. Luke figured the two brothers were going to keep searching for Jordan while Zach wanted to see what he and Finn uncovered.

Sophie stepped up to Zach and squeezed his forearm. He shot her a tight smile that faded quickly. A dart of jealousy flashed through Luke. Not at the interaction between the two. Sophie's actions were those of a concerned friend, nothing more.

Instead, the jealousy—and slight bit of shame—came from the fact that she *was* Zach's friend. Before yesterday, Luke wouldn't have been able to say that she was anything more than a passing acquaintance. Someone he'd known on a professional basis. Although, if he was honest, he'd admit he found her attractive and had had a few wishful thoughts about her being closer to his age. But he wouldn't have called her a friend. Before today.

"Luke?" Finn said. "What are you thinking?"

Luke blinked and focused. "It's been wiped clean," he said softly.

"Looks like it. Someone trying to hide prints? Evidence?"

"That's what my gut says. But I want to let Bruno take a sniff. He's been trained in more than just finding dead bodies. Let's see if he alerts to anything."

"Like what?"

Luke shrugged. "I don't know. If it's been wiped clean, there may be traces of evidence left that we can't see, but Bruno can smell."

"Like blood," Finn said flatly.

"Yeah."

Finn nodded. Luke avoided eye contact with those watching, got Bruno and brought him over to the vehicle. "Go, boy," he said softly. "Search."

Bruno hopped into the vehicle and went to work. His head bobbed and weaved as he examined the front seat, then Luke let him out and into the very back where Snapper would have been in the kennel box. Bruno took one sniff near the front of the box and sat.

"He found something," Luke said.

"What?"

Luke climbed in and used the light on his phone

to illuminate the area Bruno had alerted to. He sucked in an audible breath.

"What is it?" Finn asked.

"A dark stain. On the bottom of the door. It's dried, but it could be blood. Let me get the luminol and we'll find out for sure, then see if there's any evidence of more and whether someone tried to clean it up. We'll get this sent off to the lab and processed ASAP. If it's blood, I want it compared to Jordan's."

Luke climbed out of the vehicle and shot another look over his shoulder. All three brothers stood silent, arms crossed, eyes intense. He sighed and rose. Zach raised a brow, questions all over his expression.

"Just getting something from my trunk," Luke said.

"What?" Sophie asked.

Luke hesitated.

"Spit it out, man," Zach said. "There's no way we're having secrets."

"I'm going to get some luminol to take a sample of something that could possibly be blood." Zach paled. Luke held up a hand. "It's only a small dark stain. Could be from anything. It's not enough to scare me, but we've got to process it and the rest of the vehicle."

Zach swallowed hard. Sophie's fingers curled into fists. Luke retrieved the luminol and other items he needed for the sample and passed them to Finn. If someone had cleaned up the vehicle and tried to get rid of any other blood that had spilled, Finn would find it and then CSU would take over when they arrived.

"When you're finished, we'll let one of the officers run it to the lab so they can get started on it ASAP."

"Good idea."

Ten minutes later, a uniformed officer sped away, siren wailing. Luke drew in a deep breath. "Have Noah or Carter found anything?" he asked Zach. The young man shook his head. "All right, then. I think it's time to join in with Carter and Noah and search this area again. If his vehicle is here, maybe Jordan is, too."

Unfortunately, he was deathly afraid that if Jordan was here, they were way too late to be of any help.

SIX

Sophie bit her lip and watched as the cruiser took the evidence away, then turned her attention back to the action in front of her. Luke's phone rang, and he answered it while Finn readied Abernathy to start searching.

"Right. Okay," Luke said into the phone. "Thanks, Dani." He hung up and turned to them. "Dani's gotten some surveillance video from the guy who kidnapped Sophie and says she knows how he managed to disappear after the wreck." He nodded to Finn. "We'll check it out after we're finished here."

Finn held Jordan's shirt from yesterday so Abernathy could get a good whiff of it. The dog sniffed it and stuck his nose to the ground, then in the air as he paced back and forth near Jordan's SUV.

When he caught the scent, he took off down the trail weaving back and forth on the asphalt but heading deeper into the wooded area away from the trail's entrance. Finn hoofed it after the dog, followed by Jordan's brothers.

Sophie hurried over to Luke, who stood still and silent. Watching. "What is it? Aren't we going?"

He blinked as though she'd pulled him from some deep mental place. "Yes." But instead of following the others, he walked to his vehicle, grabbed his evidence duffel from the back and let Bruno out.

"What are you doing?" she asked. "This isn't a job for Bruno. He finds dead people, not living ones."

"He needs to walk and find a tree. We'll stay far enough behind that he won't be a distraction to Abernathy."

Sophie frowned, anxiety notching up. "You think we're going to need Bruno, don't you?" she asked quietly. Tears and hysteria welled, and she squelched both with a massive dose of willpower.

"I sincerely hope not," Luke said, "but I can't deny that I have a feeling—"

"What? What kind of feeling?" Why was she asking? She already knew the answer. She supposed she wanted him to deny it.

He glanced at the trail and shook his head. "Never mind. You ready?"

"I am." The three started off at a fast clip with Bruno leading the way. "What kind of feeling?" Sophie asked again, unable to resist pressing for an answer.

"It's probably nothing."

"You don't believe that."

He shrugged.

"Fine. I don't want to speculate on that either, so let me run this by you."

"Sure. What?"

"I've been thinking," Sophie said.

"About?"

"The reason that guy decided to kidnap me. I think Gavin's right. I was in the wrong place at the wrong time. I think the guy planted that suicide note in Jordan's folder and when I walked in to question him, he realized he was caught. Kidnapping me was a spur-of-the-moment, desperate act of someone who didn't want it found out that he was there. Thankfully, you came along when you did."

"It's a little soon right now, but I'll follow up on the letter in a couple of hours and see if the lab was able to find any prints."

"Please."

She dodged a tree limb as Bruno continued to mirror a similar path that Abernathy had taken, weaving and sniffing. It didn't take long to catch up to the others, who'd stopped.

Finn looked up when they approached and shook his head. "Abernathy's lost the scent. I'll need a minute to help him get it back."

Luke held Bruno back when the dog wanted to lurch forward. "Easy, boy."

Sophie frowned, watching, keeping her thoughts to herself.

Noah sighed. "We'll keep going and see if we find anything out of the ordinary. Radio us if Abernathy catches the scent again."

Finn nodded, and Noah, Carter and Zach continued to trek the path, leaving Finn, Sophie, Luke and the dogs alone. The whomp-whomp-whomp of blades cutting through the air reached her and she looked up through a break in the trees just in time to see a helicopter make a pass.

"The media's here," she said.

"How'd they find out so fast?" Luke muttered.

"There are a lot of cop cars here," Sophie said. "They know something's going on, but probably not the details."

"Then we need to get going on this. It won't be a secret for much longer." Finn held the bag with the shirt out to Abernathy once more.

"I think that Jordan was forced to write that note," Sophie said, picking up her earlier train of thought. "Katie was absolutely right. If someone threatened her or someone he loved, Jordan would have just written the note with the intention of tearing it up later after he explained what happened."

"I agree," Luke said, "but my question is why? What's the reason behind it? The motive?"

Finn glanced at her, started to say something, then went silent.

"What?" she asked. "Now's not the time to withhold your thoughts."

"Could I say something without you two thinking the worst of me or getting mad?" he asked.

She glanced at Luke, who shrugged, then studied Finn for a second before nodding. "Okay."

"While I think that what you've just described is a likely scenario, how well do we know Jordan? Any of us? After all, he wouldn't be the first cop to hide his emotions, his true feelings, under a layer of professionalism."

Sophie scowled. "Not Jordan. I saw him day in and day out. If he was depressed or struggling with something, I would have noticed." She paused. "Or Katie would have mentioned it. We're good friends and she wouldn't keep something like that from me."

"I agree with Sophie," Luke said. "If she says Jordan was fine emotionally, then he was." He swept an arm out. "And besides, all of this screams foul play."

Sophie shot Luke a grateful smile. She appreciated his support and faith in her. It drew her like a magnet, but she couldn't help a small silent caution to her heart. Luke acted like he took her seriously, but not many men did because of her age and appearance that made her seem even younger. So, for now, while she had hope that Luke saw her as someone who knew what she was talking about professionally, she'd keep her guard up on the personal front.

Finn nodded and controlled the suddenly eager dog pulling at the lead. "I'm just trying to cover all the bases. Truly, I don't think Jordan killed himself. I just think, as cops, we need to look at all angles."

"I know," Sophie muttered. "But not this time. I was kidnapped by the guy who planted the note, remember?"

Abernathy pulled harder and Finn gave a grin of satisfaction. "We're back on the scent. Let's go find our boss and bring him home."

Sophie and Luke let Finn and Abernathy get a short lead before following after them. Sophie sent up silent prayers and kept her eyes open for anything that might lead them to Jordan. Abernathy led them off the jogging trail, his tail wagging.

Bruno lifted his head and swiveled left. He pulled on his lead and Luke sucked in a breath. "No," he whispered. Sophie's heart clenched. She met Luke's gaze and the stark agony there terrified her.

"Luke?"

Without a word, he followed Bruno off the trail, stepping over the underbrush and around a dense set of trees. Sophie followed, doing her best to ignore her pounding heart.

And then Bruno found a small path that led around another thick copse of bushes and trees.

He followed it and disappeared from sight. And the leash went slack.

Luke pulled up short. "Stay back, Sophie."

"What does that mean, Luke? Why isn't he moving?" But she knew why. Bruno wasn't moving because he was sitting—his alert that he'd found a body. She caught up to Luke and grasped his arm. "It doesn't mean it's Jordan."

"I know. I'm going to find out. Just stay put." Luke vanished.

But she couldn't. She followed him, her eyes landing first on Bruno, who sat facing them. When she looked behind him, she let out a small cry. Dressed in his jogging clothes, Jordan sat back against a tree trunk, eyes open, staring at nothing.

Luke bit back his own cry but couldn't suppress the low moan of grief.

"Jordy!"

Sophie's piercing cry turned him around just in time to catch her around the waist as she hurled herself toward Jordan's body. "No, Sophie, you can't do anything. He's gone." He pulled her into a hug, holding her against his chest while she wailed. "He's gone," he whispered against her ear.

And had been for a while judging from the color of his skin and sightless gaze. But Luke would check. He had to. He pressed Sophie's face into his chest, feeling the shudders wracking her.

"I'm going to see if there's a pulse." Even though he knew there wouldn't be, but some small sliver of hope urged him to try. "Stay here for a second, please? I mean it. We can't mess up the scene. And…call the others, will you?"

She nodded, and he released her, pressing Bruno's leash into her hand. From his bag, he pulled little blue booties and slipped them over his shoes to prevent tracking any foreign evidence into the area. With one last look at the trail, expecting to see Jordan's brothers appear any moment, he turned to make his way to his boss, noting the landscape, the trampled undergrowth and broken tree limbs.

It looked like Jordan had just walked over, sat down…and died. A long groove in the ground looked like someone had dragged a stick, then stopped at Jordan's resting place.

Kneeling in front of the man who'd been more than a boss, one he'd considered a friend, Luke clamped his lips together and pressed his fingers against Jordan's neck, then his limp wrist.

Nothing.

The fact that his skin was cold to the touch told him Jordan had been dead for a while. Lividity had come and gone, which meant he'd probably been dead shortly after they realized he'd gone missing.

Luke dropped his chin to his chest to get his raging emotions under control. Once again, he was too late. His mother had died because he'd been late—killed by a carjacker when he was eight years old. He still blamed himself when he thought about it too long. And now Jordan. *Too late, too late, too late.*

"Luke?"

Sophie's wavering voice brought him to his feet. He turned to find Zach, Noah and Carter standing back, faces twisted in stunned grief, but with faint hope that Luke would find a pulse. Finn held Abernathy back, ordering the dog to sit, his own anxious gaze matching those of Jordan's brothers.

Luke met Sophie's eyes, then the brothers', and gave a slight shake of his head.

"No!" Zach's wail echoed through the trees. He turned and punched the nearest trunk. Then clasped it and pressed his forehead against it. Noah wrapped his arms around his younger brother. Carter didn't move, his gaze locked on Jordan's body. His mouth worked, but no sound emerged. He took a step toward Jordan.

Luke went to Carter and gripped his friend's bicep, stopping his forward momentum. "I can't let you go to him," Luke said hoarsely. "We have to protect the scene." He left out the word *crime* but knew it was implied.

Carter spun away to drop his head. His shoulders gave a violent shudder, then went still. When he turned back, his reddened eyes burned into Luke's. "Get this investigation going, Luke.

Please," he whispered, the raw anguish searing Luke's heart.

Noah stepped forward, jaw hard, eyes harder. "I don't know what happened, but my brother didn't kill himself and we need you to help prove it."

"Of course." Luke nodded and cleared his throat. "Finn, secure the scene." He didn't recognize his own grief-ravaged voice, but they needed to act. Jordan deserved it.

All three brothers now stood next to one another, their eyes on Jordan. And all three held themselves back from rushing to the man, knowing they'd destroy any evidence that might be there to tell them what happened. "Carter?" Luke asked. The man shifted his gaze to Luke. "Can you, Noah and Zach search for Snapper? If Jordan's here, so's Snapper."

With a jerky nod, Carter turned. He directed his other two brothers to follow.

Zach shook his head. "I'm not leaving him." He crossed his arms and kept his eyes locked on Jordan.

Carter started to say something, but Noah put out a hand. "It's okay."

Noah and Carter took off down the trail, seemingly grateful to be able to focus on something other than the soul-crushing despair. Zach stayed put, still as a statue, his eyes locked on his brother.

Sliding his hands around Sophie's biceps, Luke grasped them in a gentle grip. "Sophie?"

She looked up, tears streaking her ashen cheeks. "I'm going to call it in," he said. "Okay?"

She nodded. "Yes. You have to call it in."

Her automated response came from shock and he gave her a second before he squeezed her arms. She drew in a shuddering breath.

"I need you to wait on the trail," he said, "and direct the medical examiner and crime scene unit this way when they get here," he said. "It shouldn't take CSU long since they're working on the vehicle, but the ME has to have a first look. Okay?"

She nodded again, her eyes fixed on his. Trusting him. Willing to follow his lead. His throat tightened. He didn't deserve that look. Shoving aside the unwelcome wave of self-pity, he cleared the lump from his throat. "We've got to keep it together for Jordan, okay? Can you do that? Can you help me?" He paused and drew in a steadying breath. "Because if you lose it, I will, too."

With a slow nod, Sophie straightened her shoulders and swiped her cheeks. "I can do that. For Jordan—and you." She functioned on autopilot, her mind grappling with disbelief and sorrow.

But she'd keep it together. For now. Time passed in a blur of crime scene tape, pictures, the medical examiner's appearance and the subsequent removal of Jordan's body in the black bag. Sophie watched them go. So many questions— very few answers.

"Anyone find Snapper?" Luke asked her as Finn stepped up to join them. The crime scene unit had appeared to do their job and Sophie watched them carefully—as though just her presence would ensure their accuracy and professionalism.

"No," Sophie said. The three of them stood about ten yards away from where the CSU worked, surrounded by trees and other spring greenery. But for her, the place had lost its beauty and it would forever have the dark stench of death stamped on it. "Which means someone took him," she added. Finn raised a brow and she shrugged. "Snapper was Jordan's shadow. That dog would have stayed by Jordan and probably barked his head off until someone came to investigate. You know that as well as I do. If Snapper isn't here, then someone took him. It's as simple as that."

"And just as complicated," Luke said softly.

"Yeah."

Finn sighed. "I'll go talk to Jordan's brothers and fill them in."

He left, and Luke turned a concerned gaze on her. "Are you going to be okay?"

"In time." She rubbed her arms, the goose bumps there having nothing to do with the weather. "I'll grieve like we all will and I know eventually, his loss will hurt less, but for now..."

"Yeah."

"The healing process will go faster if we could catch Jordan's killer."

"We don't know that there is a killer," he reminded her gently.

Meeting his gaze, she offered him a sad smile. "Yes, we do."

He looked away with a short nod. "The medical examiner said she couldn't see any outward reason for Jordan's death. No bullet holes, no trauma, nothing. So, let's wait for the official word before we call it murder, okay?"

"Okay."

"But," he said with a sidelong glance at her, "we're going to start investigating like it's a murder. Just in case. We don't want to lose any time or momentum. If it turns out not to be, then so be it."

"Good."

"And we need to find Snapper. We'll get some flyers printed and posted. Maybe offer a reward for his return."

"Good idea," she said softly.

"Hey, Luke?" Finn called. "Can you come over here a second?"

"Sure." Luke squeezed her shoulder and left to join Finn.

Sophie stayed put, thinking. What was she missing? Did she know something that would help find Jordan's killer and she just didn't know she knew? When racking her brain produced nothing, she spun to head back to the vehicle. There was nothing more she could do here.

A loud crack echoed through the air and a puff

of wooded undergrowth littered her ankles. Sophie jerked to a stop.

"Sophie! Get down!"

She dropped just as another bullet slammed into the tree trunk beside her. And then Luke was there, his body covering hers, his weapon in hand, looking for a target.

Officers swarmed past, each one taking care to use the trees as cover while searching for the shooter.

Luke's hand closed over hers and pulled. "Stay behind a tree!"

Sophie ducked, heart pounding. She grasped the trunk and knelt, trying to make herself as small a target as possible. Shouts from the other officers reached her as they quickly formulated a plan to catch the shooter.

And then Luke was beside her, his hand on her shoulder. "Head to the vehicle, Sophie. Bruno, heel!"

A motorcycle roared, then the engine faded as the three of them raced down the path toward the SUV. With a click of the remote, the back door opened. Bruno shot into his area and Luke reached around Sophie to shove her into the passenger side. When he landed in the driver's seat with a grunt, Sophie turned, heart thudding, hands shaking.

"Are you okay?" he demanded.

"Yes. I... I think so. Someone was shooting at me...or us?"

"He was definitely shooting at someone, but you're safe now. There's no way he's still around here with so many officers on his tail. They'll catch him."

"And if they don't?" She couldn't help the small squeak that slipped from her throat.

Reaching across the console, he pulled her into a hug and she buried her face into his shoulder for the second time that day.

"They will. I'm so sorry this is happening to you. You don't deserve this, Sophie."

She sniffed and squeezed her eyes against the flood of tears that wanted to fall. Crying could come later. Right now, she had to think. "Why does he keep coming back?"

"Because you saw him."

"But I didn't get a good look! Even when we were in the car racing through the streets, he had the baseball hat and sunglasses on. I don't think I could even pick him out of a lineup."

"Yeah, same here. But either he doesn't realize that, or it doesn't matter to him." He held her tighter. "I'll protect you, Sophie, I promise."

"But who's going to protect you?"

A knock on the window pulled them apart. Finn stood there. Luke lowered the window.

"We spotted him, but he got away," Finn said, his gaze bouncing between the two of them.

"The motorcycle?"

"Yeah. We couldn't pinpoint exactly where he was shooting from, but after he took his shots and realized we were coming, he hopped on and hightailed it out of here. I've already released a description, but it's not much so I'm not holding out too much hope."

Luke nodded. "All right, I'm going to take Sophie home. Keep me updated."

"Of course."

Once Finn was gone, Sophie shook her head. "You can't take me home yet."

"Why not?"

"I need to at least be there when Katie gets the news."

Luke took her hand. "Of course. I'll take you to see her."

Her phone rang. "Hello?"

"It's Noah, Sophie. We're headed to Katie's and were wondering if you could be there."

"I was just heading that way."

"I think the media is heading for the house. See if you can beat them there and keep her from hearing it from anyone but one of us."

"Me? But—" How would she manage to do that?

"She'll need you," Noah said, his voice hoarse."

"I… Okay. I'll do my best."

"Thank you."

Frankly, she wondered if she'd be able to even look Katie in the eye when she saw her, but she'd have to try. For Katie.

SEVEN

Luke's heart still pounded with shock and grief and he had to wonder if the feelings would ease anytime soon. He doubted it but did his best to focus on Sophie. "Tell me how you and Katie came to be such good friends?" he asked as he headed toward the Jamesons' house in Rego Park.

"When I started working for Jordan, he introduced me to Katie right away, said he had a feeling we'd be good friends." She gave him a half smile. "He took us both to lunch one day and we hit it off immediately."

"He had good intuition about a lot of things."

"True. Anyway, sometimes when Katie would come in to the office to see Jordan, she'd have to wait if he was on the phone or in a meeting that went long. We'd wind up chatting, and eventually, we started going to lunch together a few times a week—especially if Jordan couldn't go."

"Sounds nice."

"It was." She blinked at the sudden rush of

tears once again. "I can't believe the timing of this. It's unbelievable."

He frowned at her and she pressed her fingers against her lips. What did the timing of Jordan's death have to do with anything? It's not like there would be a better time for him to die, would there? Luke had the feeling that wasn't the way she meant her words to sound. Instead, he figured she knew something she wasn't telling and he didn't like it. Instead of pressing her, he drove through the streets of Rego Park, turning onto Furmanville Avenue and past the St. John Cemetery, then onto Woodhaven Boulevard, all the while looking for a parking spot. He could use the BFK parking garage, but that was about a mile and a half from the Jamesons' home and he didn't want Sophie exposed for the length of time it would take to walk from the garage. Then again, he could just drop her at the door of the house and go find a spot, but that would entail leaving her.

Finally, he wedged the SUV at the end of the block on Fitchett Street and cut the engine. When he turned to look at her, the devastation on her face grabbed his heart in a vice grip. He took her hand in his. "I'll be there, too, okay? We'll all be there and be her support. Whatever she needs."

Sophie nodded, opened her door and stepped out of the vehicle. Luke did the same and released Bruno from his area. The dog trotted beside them as they worked their way up the sidewalk. Luke kept his eyes open, watching the surrounding area. He hadn't mentioned it to Sophie, but he'd been looking for more than a parking spot while he'd been driving up and down the streets.

And while he saw nothing that set off his alarm bells, he couldn't help the feeling that someone was out there. Watching and waiting for the chance to get to Sophie. The thought propelled him closer to her and he wrapped an arm around her shoulders.

She glanced up but didn't pull away. Seconds later, they approached the front door. Officers stood outside the home. A protective measure for Katie just in case whatever caused Jordan to disappear—and die—was a threat to Katie. Luke knew they were there, as well, out of concern and support for the wife of their chief.

He nodded to each of them.

"Any word on the chief?" one asked.

"I can't say anything right now," Luke said, "but you'll be hearing something soon." No way was anyone else finding out about Jordan's death before the man's wife.

"Luke. Sophie!"

He turned to see Noah, Carter and Zach hurrying toward them. Luke stepped back and allowed the brothers to take the lead. Noah opened the door and they made their way to Katie and Jordan's apartment.

Zach knocked.

When Katie opened the door, her red-rimmed eyes met Zach's, then bounced from person to person until they finally landed on Sophie, who stood slightly in front of the brothers. Luke frowned at Katie's almost translucent appearance.

"What is it?" she asked. "Did you find him?"

Zach drew in a deep breath and nodded.

"Well, what?"

No one spoke. Finally, Sophie took her friend's hand in hers and led her back through the foyer and into the den. "Let's sit down."

Katie obediently followed Sophie to the couch and sank onto it. "It's obviously not good. So, what? Which hospital is he in? How bad is it?"

Noah stepped forward and cleared his throat. "He's gone, Katie," Noah said.

"He's…" Sophie glanced at Luke and the others. She swallowed. For a moment, Katie simply stared at her brother-in-law. "Gone? Gone where?"

Sophie shook her head and Noah gripped her fingers. "He's dead, Katie. He's…dead." He choked on the last word and turned away.

Again, Katie stayed rock still for a good ten seconds, then tears filled her eyes to spill over her lashes and streak her cheeks. "No," she whispered. Her face crumpled, and Sophie leaped forward to pull her friend into an embrace while Luke looked away and pressed fingers to his burning eyes.

This wasn't the first time he'd had to be present or tell someone a family member had died, but it sure was the hardest. "I'm sorry, Katie," he whispered.

Katie sobbed into Sophie's shoulder for what seemed like an eternity. Finally, she pulled back and Sophie pressed tissues into the woman's hand. Luke didn't know where she'd gotten them, but he was beginning to understand that that was Sophie. Always prepared. Even for this.

"It's on the news," Zach said, his voice rough. He glanced up from his phone. "Someone leaked it." He looked ready to find the person responsible and let them have it.

"We were worried about that and got here as fast as we could," Luke said. "How far away are your parents?" he asked.

"They should be here anytime now," Carter said.

"Do they know?"

"Yes." Noah raked a hand over his head. "Once we realized it was on the news, we had no choice but to break it to them over the phone."

"I'm sorry."

A sharp cry escaped Katie and she broke away from Sophie to dart down the hallway.

"Katie?" Zach called. His sister-in-law ignored him.

Sophie's tear-filled eyes met Luke's for a brief second, then she hurried after her friend.

Sophie stopped at the bathroom door. The sounds of Katie being sick reached her and she closed her eyes to offer up a silent prayer for her grieving friend. When it sounded as if the episode was over, Sophie knocked.

"Come in."

Katie sat on the floor, her back against the wall, eyes closed. "What am I going to do without him?" she whispered as another tear slid down to drop off her jaw.

Sophie sighed and lowered herself beside her friend. "You'll go on and you'll raise his baby to know that his or her daddy was a hero."

Katie gave a slight nod, but her tears never stopped flowing.

"And," Sophie said, "it might be a good idea to tell everyone about the baby. Not only will it give everyone hope that Jordy will live on in his child, but you need the support, someone to go to your doctor's appointments with you and hold your hand through all of this."

"You haven't mentioned it?"

"Of course not. That's not my news to share."

"No. It was *ours*." Her eyes opened, and anger flashed. "Mine and Jordy's. And now that's been ripped away from us. Why?"

Sophie gripped her friend's cold fingers and squeezed. "I don't know, Katie. It's not fair."

"No, it's not." She sighed, and her shoulders drooped, surprising Sophie that the sudden surge of anger vanished in a flash to be replaced with raw grief once more. "I'll tell them after the funeral," Katie said. "But…if it becomes necessary for someone to know, then you have my blessing."

"Thanks. It might very well be necessary." She really thought Luke should know if only to fully convince him that Jordan would never take his own life. "But why not tell everyone now? It would be such joyous news in the midst of all of this tragedy." Wouldn't it?

Katie swiped a tear. "I don't know. Do you really think so? That it will bring them joy or just heighten the loss and the grief because they all know how much Jordan would have loved this baby and now he'll never get to—" She pressed the heels of her hands to her eyes.

Sophie bit her lip. "I truly don't know."

"Jordy and I wanted to keep this just between us for a while," Katie said, dropping her hands into her lap. "So we could savor the idea—and make sure the pregnancy was going like it should—not that we had any reason to think otherwise." She gave a small shrug. "But it was fun. It was our secret." Another tear dripped off her chin and she nodded. "All right. I'll tell them in a few minutes."

Silence fell between them and for several minutes they sat there while Katie worked on getting her tears under control and Sophie wondered what the future would hold for her friend.

"How did he die?" Katie finally asked. "Who killed him? Because I know it wasn't self-inflicted."

"I don't know. I saw him," Sophie said softly. "And…"

"Tell me. Please."

"He looked peaceful. Like he'd taken a walk in the woods and found a comfortable spot to sit while he contemplated the future." No need to mention his open, staring eyes. "There wasn't a bullet hole or any blood except for a trace amount found in his vehicle. And it's very possible it wasn't his. The medical examiner will know more once she's finished with the…everything."

"The autopsy."

"Yes." Sophie didn't want to say the word in relation to Jordan. The fact that Katie had done so was a testament to her strength. Strength that Sophie was going to have to find and emulate.

"Where's Snapper?" Katie asked. "Did you find him?"

"No."

Katie groaned and lowered her forehead to her knees. "He should have been right there with Jordy. He wouldn't have left him willingly."

"I agree. We've already talked about that. Everyone's searching for him now. And now that it's all over the news, I think they're going to print up some flyers and put them out along the biking trail and around the park."

A knock on the door pulled them to their feet.

"Everything okay in there?" Zach asked. "Sorry, that's a dumb question. I know everything's not okay. Is there anything you need? Anything we can do?"

"They must be feeling pretty helpless out there," Katie said.

"Probably, but you deal with this however you need to. They'll wait," Sophie said.

"No, it's okay." Katie swiped her face, then rose to wash her hands. Taking a deep breath, she faced the door. "We're coming," she called. She opened the door and Sophie followed her and Zach down the hall to the kitchen, where an older couple sat at the table, expressions drawn, cheeks wet with their tears. They rose.

"Hello, Mr. and Mrs. Jameson," Sophie said while Katie slipped into her mother-in-law's arms.

"Hello, Sophie." Mr. Jameson hugged her. Hard. His desperate grief reached inside her and ripped at the fragile hold she had on her emotions.

One by one, Jordan's brothers hugged Katie, then led their parents and Katie into the living area.

Luke stayed behind. "Can I help do something?"

"You can make all of this go away or wake me up from the nightmare," Sophie said softly, pulling plastic cups and plates from under the cabinet near the refrigerator.

"I wish I could."

"I know."

She rummaged through the refrigerator, pulling leftover containers and lifting the lids, sniffing… and mostly tossing into the trash.

"What are you doing?" he asked, mystified.

"As soon as people hear, they're going to be arriving in droves. Jordy and Katie are…were…a part of a large couples Bible study. They'll come to offer their sympathy and they'll bring food. We'll need room for it. There's another refrigerator and freezer outside on the porch, as well."

Luke stood, held silent by her resilience and her thoughtfulness. "You're amazing," he finally said softly. She was hurting, grieving, just like the rest of them—and yet she was putting everyone else first.

She paused and offered him a small smile. "I'm not that amazing. It helps to stay busy, to focus on something besides my shattered heart."

"Yeah." He paused. "What can I do to help?"

From the pantry, she pulled out a few water bottles and set them on the counter. "I don't know. Nothing, really."

"Sophie?"

She turned to see Katie in the doorway. The woman hurried over to her and grabbed her in a hug much like the one Mr. Jameson had given Sophie earlier.

Luke nodded to the door, indicating he was going to give them privacy.

* * *

Sophie hugged Katie back. "What is it? Here, take a water bottle. As many tears as you've cried, you need to hydrate."

A giggle slipped from Katie and she slapped a hand over her mouth. "How can I laugh at that? Something is wrong with me if I can laugh at a time like this."

"Nothing is wrong with you other than elevated hormones. And dare I say it, but Jordy would be the first one to tell you to laugh."

"Thank you," Katie whispered and gave her another hug. "I can't thank you enough for just being here. I love my in-laws, but sometimes they can overwhelm a girl a bit."

"I'm here anytime you need me, Katie. You'll get through this. It's going to be hard and there are going to be some dark days ahead, but we'll get there. We have to," she whispered, releasing her friend and gripping her hands once more. "It's what Jordy would want."

Katie nodded. "You're right. It is what he'd want. He'd want us to be happy and to enjoy life and laughter again. Just keep reminding me of that when I'm deep in the pit of despair and missing him desperately, okay?"

"I promise." It would be a good reminder for Sophie, too.

"Okay, I'm going to put on my strong face and go back into the den and tell them about the baby."

"Good."

After yet another hug, Katie left, and Sophie grabbed two water bottles and went in search of Luke. She found him in the sunroom, hands shoved into his pockets, staring out into the backyard. Bruno lay stretched out on the large throw rug, his watchful eyes following her.

"Katie's with her in-laws now. I think she's going to be all right. Eventually."

"She will. It'll be hard, but she'll get there. It may not seem like it now, but we all will." A pause. "I don't understand," he said softly.

"Understand what?"

"This whole thing. I keep thinking about him. Just sitting there under the tree. No sign of foul play, nothing."

"Have they found his phone?"

"No, but that doesn't mean he didn't leave it somewhere."

"Not Jordan. And especially not now."

He turned. "Where does this unwavering faith come from? How are you so sure?"

"I...just know. Without a doubt."

Luke ran a hand over his chin. "Okay, well, let's say you're right and Jordan didn't kill himself. I truly don't think so, but I'll admit to some lingering doubts. However..."

"However...?" she asked.

"If it wasn't suicide then that means his death was either due to some crazy undiagnosed medical issue, like a heart condition or a brain aneurysm or—"

"Or it was murder," she said. "And since he'd just had a checkup not too long ago, I'm going with murder." Although, she admitted silently, some things could be missed even in a thorough checkup. But still…something in her said Jordan's death wasn't an accident or a medical mishap.

Luke nodded. "I was inclined to believe that, too—until I saw him. I took a good look at him, Sophie. There were no wounds or any evidence of a traumatic injury."

She sighed and rubbed her eyes. "Well, I guess we'll just have to wait and see what the medical examiner says." She paused and handed him one of the bottles of water.

"Thanks."

"Sure. So, what's next?"

"What's next is," Luke said with a heaviness that made her heart hurt even more, "they plan a funeral and we find out why our healthy, happy friend died."

He twisted the cap off the bottle and took a long swig. She could tell he was still troubled and even knowing she couldn't really help, she had to try. "Tell me," she said softly.

"I'm just thinking."

"About Jordan, of course."

"Of course." He gave a short laugh, one without humor. "I can't stop thinking about him. I keep running everything through my mind over and over. It's like a loop and I can't seem to find the stop button."

"You're wondering if you could have saved him."

Luke jerked, his eyes locked on hers. "Yes, but how...?"

"Because I'm wondering the same thing. Well, not if you personally could have, but if any of us could have. What did we miss? If it was murder, who had it in for him?" She glanced into the den, where Katie and her brothers-in-law sat speaking in low tones. "And does someone now have it in for Katie?"

Luke took her hands in his. "I know you're worried for Katie. I am, too. But she has four male protectors in there and a mother-in-law who thinks of her as her own daughter. I think we need to turn our focus on you—and who has it in for you."

EIGHT

Sophie shivered at his ominous reminder and he grimaced. He knew she'd been working hard to put the incidents aside in order to be there for Katie, but he also needed her to stay alert and watchful. "Are you ready to go?"

She nodded. "I'll check with Katie and make sure she's all right with me leaving."

While Sophie was doing that, Luke stepped into the foyer and called their tech guru, breathing a sigh of relief when she answered on the first ring. "Hi, Dani."

"Hi, Luke."

"Any news?"

"Like what?"

"Like security footage of Vanderbilt Parkway."

Keyboard keys clicked in the background. "I just got it in, believe it or not. I haven't really had a chance to go through it yet."

"Want an extra pair of eyes?"

"Always. But I'll be reviewing it while you're on the way."

"Thirty minutes?"

"I'll be here. Gotta go. Bye." She hung up.

Dani was fabulously good at her job even if her phone etiquette could use a little work. He went looking for Sophie to let her know he was ready and found her in the kitchen with Katie. The two had their heads bent together and were whispering. He cleared his throat and they both jumped as though guilty of some conspiracy. "Uh, sorry. If you need more time."

"No," Katie said. "It's okay. I was just explaining something to Sophie. Thank you for everything."

"Sure."

She headed back to join her family and Sophie turned her gaze on him. "So, we're headed to headquarters?" Sophie asked, her brow still furrowed from the conversation he'd just interrupted.

"If that's all right."

"It's more than all right. At least I feel like we're doing something proactive that might lead us to discover what happened to Jordan instead of sitting around waiting on…everything."

They found the others and said their goodbyes with Katie promising to call should she need anything. Zach, Noah and Carter all wanted to go, too, when they realized the footage was available.

"It's better if you don't," Luke said. "You three

can't be anywhere near the investigation on this. Should Jordan's death be due to something other than an accident or a health-related issue—"

"Like murder?" Carter snapped.

"Yes," Luke said evenly. "Like murder. If that's the case, you don't want to do anything that would jeopardize us getting a conviction once we catch the person responsible."

Zach's jaw tightened, and Noah laid a hand on his shoulder without taking his eyes from Luke. "You'll let us know what you know?"

"As soon as I know it."

Noah gave a short nod and Sophie followed Luke out to the SUV. A light rain misted them. "I hope this doesn't interfere with gathering any evidence around the crime scene."

"They'll have known it was coming and prepared for it." And worked fast.

Luke drove to headquarters and found a spot on the street, thankfully not too far from the entrance. "You ready?" he asked Sophie.

"I guess so." She bit her lip and sighed. He didn't have to be a genius to know it was going to be devastating walking into that building when Jordan never would again.

When he let Bruno out, the dog shook himself and trotted toward the three-story building. Luke and Sophie followed. Luke kept her between him and the suite of offices to their left as they walked down the sidewalk.

If there had been a better way to get into headquarters without exposing Sophie to the outside, he would have used it. Having no choice, he did his best to use his body as a shield, although he'd admit to breathing a sigh of relief when they reached the double glass doors that led into the main lobby area. He punched in the code that allowed them access and stepped inside.

Luke was almost as comfortable in this building as he was in his own home. Bruno was, too. Mostly because of the treats Luke kept in the bottom drawer of his desk. Since his reward for finding a cadaver was playtime with a tennis ball, the treats wouldn't confuse him.

The receptionist, Officer Patricia Knowles, sat behind the large U-shaped desk where she kept tabs on the comings and goings of the handlers and their K-9s—and answered the never-ending ringing phone.

Once inside the lobby, Luke nodded to Patricia, whose eyes went wide at their entrance, but she simply threw them a wave before pressing the button on her headset to answer the phone.

"She was surprised to see us," Sophie said.

"Jordan was just found a few hours ago. No doubt she thought we'd still be with the others."

"Which is where I'd love to be, but if this can help us find Jordan's killer, then this is where I need to be."

"Exactly."

Luke headed for the large open area with cubicles that separated the handlers' desks and gave them a modicum of privacy.

Somber eyes followed him, and he knew each person wanted to stop him and ask him about Jordan, but they respected his body language and turned their attention to Sophie. One by one, she hugged each officer.

While she spent time giving and receiving condolences and fielding questions that had no answers, Luke stopped at his desk to retrieve a treat for Bruno, who wolfed it down. For a moment, he leaned against his desk and closed his eyes. He wanted to pray, but the heaviness in his soul had no words. Instead, he drew in a deep breath and found Bruno had settled onto the dog bed in the corner and was watching him with sympathetic dark eyes.

When he had his emotions under control, Luke exited the cubicle and nodded to Sophie, who extricated herself from the others. She walked with him past the small connecting hallway that led to Jordan's office. Just outside Jordan's office was Sophie's area. Her desk was tidy, the chair pushed in. It looked ready for her to return. He averted his eyes from Jordan's door as emotion welled once more and couldn't help noticing that Sophie did the same.

Luke led the way down the stairs. The large training center was to the left. Dani's office to the right. The door stood open and she motioned them inside. Her red-rimmed hazel eyes behind the large-framed glasses perched on her nose attested to her own emotional state. She had her curly blond hair pulled up into a messy ponytail. "How's Katie?" she asked.

"Not good, as you can imagine," Sophie said, "but she's strong. With support and love from her family and friends, she'll get through this. We all will." She felt like a broken record, but it was the only answer that fit—and offered the hope everyone needed right now. Including herself. Maybe if she said it enough, she'd start to believe it.

Dani nodded and moved behind her desk. Monitors lined the wall in front of her. "All right, just so you know, I managed to grab the footage from the ATM across the street from where your wreck happened and your kidnapper bolted. But first, let's look at the parkway footage."

"Great," Luke said. "How'd you get it so fast?"

"I pulled in a few favors I'd been saving for the right case." She shook her head. "I didn't expect to be redeeming them on a case like this."

"I know." Luke leaned in. "Show us."

"So, here's what I managed to get from some of the surrounding security cameras. There's one right before you enter the trail. Once they were on the path, it gets a little trickier. Fortunately, there's a study being done on the feasibility of expanding the parkway, so I've got a bit more to work with.

They'd placed some counters along the pathway that are triggered every time someone passes by. I don't know how accurate they are, but I think it gives a good idea of the use of the place. Anyway, I've paused it at the place where things get interesting. In spite of the darkness, you can make out what's going on pretty well. Just not who the person is in the video, unfortunately."

A few clicks on the keyboard brought images up on the monitor closest to Luke. "This is the footage from this morning," Dani said. "There wasn't any sign of him on the camera the day he actually disappeared." The footage began to play. For a moment, there was nothing, then Jordan's SUV came into view, just barely on the side of the screen. The driver exited, wearing a hoodie over a baseball cap, along with dark sunglasses. "How can he see with those on?" Sophie whispered.

"Probably put them on just before exiting the vehicle," Dani said.

The driver went to the back and pulled out a long pole. "What's he doing?" Luke asked.

"You'll see."

He attached a piece of cloth to the end, turned and lifted the pole toward the camera. The man's sleeve rode up and Luke caught sight of something on the person's arm. Then the camera went blank.

"What's the point of that?" Sophie asked. "Why try to make it look like a suicide if you're going to let yourself get caught on camera covering the lens? That doesn't make sense."

"Unless it was Jordan," Dani said. "But I'm pretty sure it wasn't him." She returned to the part where the man lifted the pole. "There. See that?" Dani zoomed in. "A tattoo of some sort. I can't make out the design, though, so there's no way to run it through the tattoo-ID software."

"It's not Jordan," Sophie said. "He doesn't have a tattoo. So, again, why would this guy allow himself to get caught on camera?"

"I don't think he realized he was within camera range," Dani said. "See where he parked?" She rewound the footage. "That's right on the edge of the parking lot. He approached the camera off to the side when he covered it. These cameras are wide-angle, though. I think he just miscalculated."

"You may be right," Luke said. "I know we need to wait for the autopsy results for an official cause of death, but this is clearly a murder however it was done. It's obvious from the note that he's trying to set up Jordan's death as a suicide, but he sure did a lousy job. Other than the token action of leaving Jordan's vehicle there to make it look like he drove himself to the park, there's no other sign that this is a suicide. What did he kill himself with? There are no pills, no evidence of any drugs, nothing."

"No one ever said criminals had to be smart," Sophie muttered.

"True enough." He glanced at Dani. "Is that it?"

"No, not totally. Take a look at this."

Another monitor blipped to life. "Like I said, there's a study being done on the path. These are the monitors that track how many people are using the path. Last night, there was nothing from 1:00 a.m. until movement at 3:20 a.m. Then at 3:25 a.m., more movement, then nothing until around 5:16 when two joggers went for their morning run."

"So, what does that tell us?" Luke asked.

"I cross-referenced that information against the security footage at the entrance to the parkway. There's no record of anyone entering around that 3:20 time on foot other than the guy who covered up the camera."

"Anyone could have entered from anywhere along the path."

"I know. But then one person exited at 3:40 at this point of the trail and this is what I got from one of the security cameras along the overpass." She clicked a few more keys. "It's two miles away from where Jordan and his SUV were found." She froze the frame to allow them a good look at the person. "He's also dressed just like the guy who got out of Jordan's SUV."

"Did he get into a vehicle?"

"I can't tell. He kept going until he was out of camera range."

"This doesn't tell us much," Sophie said. "It's terribly disappointing."

"Let's not be so hasty to assume that," Luke said. "Let's take another look. See if you spot anything that stands out. Is there anything on his clothing, shoes, hands, that could be identifiable later? Does he have a limp? A habit Anything?"

Dani played the footage again.

"He's wearing gloves," Sophie said. "This time of year that wouldn't be too suspect except maybe in the middle of the day when it warms up."

"But at night, with the temps getting into the midforties, they make sense. But that's not why he's wearing them."

Sophie shook her head. "We need to know when Jordan died," she said. "Any word about what his time of death was?"

"The ME's working on that. We should have a preliminary report soon."

"How did he get Jordan's body out there?" Sophie asked. "Jordan was a big guy. A little over six feet and all muscle. He would have weighed too much for someone to carry for very long—even for a person similar in size to Jordan."

"Good point," Luke said. "Either Jordan walked and he was killed there at the spot, or the killer had help."

"Or the killer had something to transport him in," Sophie said.

"Yeah," Luke sighed. "Or that."

Sophie shook her head. "I don't understand, though. Why put his body here where it's sure to be found rather than leaving him in a river or someplace harder to find him?"

"The killer wanted Jordan found," Luke said. "I mean, it all kind of fits with leaving the suicide note, don't you think?"

"Of course, but wait a minute," Sophie said.

"What is it?"

"Just that I think I know why he would put Jordan in that particular place. The killer thought he was being clever. Smart."

Luke tilted his head. "How so?"

"He had to be watching Jordan. Following him," she said, her voice low, thoughtful. "How else would he know what time Jordan left his home or that Jordan went running just about every single morning in that particular park?"

"He'd been spying," Luke said. "You have to be right."

"If so, then he's been planning this awhile." Sophie swallowed, suddenly nauseated at the thought. "Watching and waiting for the opportunity to strike."

"And when he got it, he took it. By planting the suicide note, then having Jordan found in a place that he was known to love..." She shrugged and swiped a tear from her cheek.

"It would back up the whole idea that he really did kill himself." His gaze snagged hers. "If you hadn't caught him planting the note, we might still be considering that it was a suicide."

"And not looking for a killer," she whispered.

"Exactly."

Luke's phone rang, and he glanced at the screen. "It's Elena, the medical examiner, I need to take it."

Luke stepped into the farthest corner of the small room and pressed the phone to his ear. "Hi, Elena. What have you got?"

"I've finished the autopsy. An initial examination of Chief Jameson shows no outward trauma. It looks like there was some damage to his heart, so I've sent off samples to be tested for various drugs, et cetera, but those won't be back for a while."

"Are you saying he had a heart attack?"

"I'm saying it's possible. There's definitely damage, but until I get the results of the tox report back, I can't say for sure what caused it."

"You can't put a rush on those results?"

A sigh reached him. "I knew Jordan, too, Luke," she said. "I'll do the best I can to hurry things along, but you know this lab stays backed up." She paused. "I'll do my best to get this expedited. He was a good man and served this city well. If he goes to the front of the line, I don't think anyone's going to argue about it."

Luke closed his eyes, grateful for the woman

who would get it done even though she made no promises. "Anything you can do would be appreciated."

"Of course."

He hung up and rubbed his eyes, then returned to Dani and Sophie, who were watching the footage one more time.

"I don't see Snapper," Sophie said.

"No, I noticed that right off," Dani said. "He could still be in the vehicle at this point, but we won't be able to know for sure since the camera's blocked."

"Anything else?" Luke asked.

"That's it for now on that one." Dani clicked a few keys on her keyboard and another file with security footage popped up onto her screen. "Okay, now, this is from the ATM across the street from where Sophie was pulled from the car by the kidnapper. You can't see the crash, but you can see the guy running away from it." She played the video. The sedan carrying Sophie and her kidnapper zipped past. A moment later, Luke pulled to a stop just past the ATM.

Dani looked at him. "Good thing you didn't park in front of it."

"I wasn't thinking about that, to be honest. I just wanted to get to Sophie."

"I know, but we're fortunate to have this." She pointed. "Okay, see that? He ran from the car and darted into the store directly across the street."

"I saw him go in there," Luke said, "and officers went after him while others traced the plates. The car was stolen, which came as a huge surprise." He couldn't help the sarcasm. He could have almost said it had been stolen without the need to run the plates. "Officers covered all the entrances and couldn't discern how he basically just disappeared."

"I think I figured that out," Dani said. She clicked a few more keys. "I looked around for some more cameras and found one inside the store. The owner was gracious enough to email me a copy of the footage. It looks like your kidnapper went into the back where the storage area is and climbed out the window and up the fire escape, then hauled himself onto the roof. I know the place was searched, but by the time officers were in the store, your guy was long gone."

She switched to another camera. "This camera was on a building opposite the one the guy ran into. Fortunately, it's at a higher level, aimed down toward the back alley—and it allows us to see a portion of the room along those connected buildings." She hit Play. "And, there he goes across the rooftops and then down the fire escape when he's almost to the end. I don't have any more footage of it, but I called the business in that last building and asked for a description of the place. From the way he described it, it's not hard to guess that the guy simply swung over the edge of the roof, planted his feet on the wrought-iron ladder and climbed down the fire escape to hit the asphalt running."

Sophie shook her head. "Well, at least we know how he got away." She looked at Luke. "So, what now?"

"Now, we bury our boss and friend and find out exactly why and how he died—and who's responsible."

Luke escorted Sophie and Bruno to the Tahoe, then climbed into the driver's seat. Something niggled at the back of his mind, but he couldn't quite put his finger on what was bothering him.

"You said something that I think we need an answer to," he said.

She turned to him. "What?"

"About Jordan and how someone managed to haul his body out to the spot where he was left. And using something to transport him."

"Yes. I can't see Jordan just walking in there and having a seat against the tree."

"He didn't."

She raised a brow and he sighed. "He'd been dead for a while by the time we found him."

"How do you know?"

"Rigor had already left his body. He wasn't stiff."

"Maybe it hadn't set in yet."

Luke shook his head. "He had on short sleeves," he said softly. "Blood had pooled under the arm that I got a good look at. That means he'd been gone awhile."

She bit her lip and looked away. "I wanted to believe we could have saved him."

"I know. We all did." He drew in a deep breath and refocused. "But what I was getting at is this. When we found Jordan, I noticed a long groove in the dirt, like someone had pulled a heavy stick through the area."

"Okay." She frowned at him. "What are you getting at?"

"What if someone used a wheelbarrow to get Jordan from his vehicle to that spot in the woods?"

Sophie tilted her head, studying him. Then gave a slow nod. "That makes sense, but there was no wheelbarrow sitting around the scene that I saw. Did you notice one?"

"No."

"And Dani showed us where the guy walked out of the area later. What did he do with the wheelbarrow?"

"Good question."

"And if he had it in the back of Jordan's vehicle, I would have thought you and Finn would have found some evidence that it had been there."

"And we didn't. Then again, the Tahoe was practically spotless except for that bit of blood and few dog hairs, which most likely belong to Snapper."

"True."

"So where would the wheelbarrow have come from and where did it go after he used it?"

They fell silent, still sitting in the running vehicle outside of headquarters. Bruno shifted so he could place his head on her shoulder with a sigh. She reached back to scratch his head and his eyes closed halfway. "He's such a good-natured dog."

"Yeah. And I made a huge goof with him the other day."

"What was that?"

"I didn't reward him for finding Jordan," he said, his voice gruff. "I didn't even think about it."

"You had other matters on your mind."

"I've never, in all my years of training and working with dogs, forgotten to reward one." Her hand closed over his and Luke let the comfort of her presence wash over him. He liked having her with him. She made the burden lighter.

"Don't beat yourself up, Luke. It's not going to ruin Bruno."

"I know, I just..." He shook his head, then met her gaze. "This has thrown me, Sophie, I'll admit it."

She nodded. "I think this has thrown everyone. I know I feel like I've been sucker punched and haven't been able to get my breath back."

"That's the most accurate description I've heard someone come up with. You're right. That's exactly how I feel. Like I haven't been able to take a deep breath since finding Jordan in the—" A memory flashed. "The vehicle at the entrance to the parkway."

"What are you talking about?"

"Maybe nothing, but I'm going to give it a shot." He grabbed his phone and called Dani while Sophie frowned her confusion. "Can you get me the number for whoever's in charge of the park maintenance and operations vehicles?"

"Vanderbilt Parkway?" Dani asked.

"Yes."

"Hold on a sec." Her keyboard clicked. "Walter Love. I'll text you the number."

His phone chimed. "Got it. Thanks."

"You think the person in that vehicle had something to do with Jordan's death?" Sophie asked.

"I don't know, but do you remember seeing it on the surveillance video?"

"No, I don't."

"That's because it was parked away from the parking lot, almost behind the camera." He dialed the number Dani had texted him, identified himself to the person who answered the phone and was put directly through to Walter Love.

"Mr. Love, this is Officer Luke Hathaway. I'm investigating an incident that happened with one of our other officers out at the Vanderbilt Parkway. This morning, there was a maintenance and operations vehicle with a trailer out there and I was wondering if you could tell me who was driving it. I'd like to question him and see if he saw anything that might help us out."

"The guy who was driving it this morning was sent out to get it because it disappeared from a work site day before yesterday."

"Disappeared?"

Sophie's gaze swiveled to his, her expression questioning.

"Yep. One of my other workers was spreading mulch and took a quick break to run to the restroom. When he came back, the truck and trailer were gone."

Luke raised a brow. "He left the keys in the ignition?"

The man coughed and cleared his throat. "Well, yeah, he did. They're not supposed to, but sometimes our guys leave them running when they're only going to be a couple of minutes—whether it's to grab a snack from a machine or whatever. I have a feeling that things are going to be changing around here after this theft incident—the only one that's ever happened, by the way. Anyway, we looked all over for it and then someone spotted it this morning, so I sent my guy out to get it about the time the cops were pulling in."

"Yeah, I remember seeing him. Listen, can you

tell me if there was a wheelbarrow in the back of it?"

"Yep, sure was."

Luke nodded, his pulse pounding a bit faster. "Great. I'm going to have officers who are in close proximity come out there and secure it. Until they get there, I'm going to need you to keep that truck and trailer under lock and key. Make sure no one touches it or uses it anymore."

"Carlos brought it back and parked it before his shift ended this morning. I'll have it secured. No one will touch it until your officers arrive."

"I'll need to speak to Carlos. Is he available?"

"I can have him in the office when you get here, or you can find him at home."

"Are you willing to give me an address over the phone?"

"If it can help catch a killer." Walter rattled it off. Then added Carlos's cell number. "See if he's home. You'll probably wake him up. But if he's not there, he's at the gym."

"Thank you so much." Luke hung up and made the arrangements for local officers and the forensics team to head out to the maintenance garage. He touched base with the other detectives working the case and filled them in. They promised to keep him in the loop if anything was discovered. When he hung up, he turned to Sophie. "I need to make a quick stop before we head back to my place."

"Of course. What's going on?"

He told her everything Walter Love had said.

"And you think Carlos might have seen something?"

"Only one way to find out."

NINE

Carlos had said he'd be home and to come on over. As she and Luke pulled to the curb of an apartment complex, Sophie sighed and rubbed her arms.

The neighborhood park across the street sat empty, devoid of children's laughter and running feet thanks to the recent surge of gang violence in the area. She'd recognized the street name from the case files sitting on Jordan's desk. Sophie shook her head and pursed her lips. Sometimes it seemed as if all of their efforts to fight crime and keep the city safe for the residents were for naught. Then again, what else were they going to do? Sit back and let the bad guys win?

Not hardly. It was an uphill battle, but one that was worth fighting.

Luke let Bruno out of his area and paused to scan his surroundings before coming around to the passenger side and opening her door.

"You see anything?" she asked.

"Nothing out of the ordinary."

He hovered close as he led the way to the glass front door. Since there was no buzzer or gate, he pulled the door open and ushered her inside with a glance back over his shoulder.

"What is it?" she asked. "You're acting nervous."

"Not nervous, just aware. And it's a feeling."

"Of?"

"Being watched, but I don't see anyone."

He'd had a feeling about Jordan, too. She shivered in spite of the warmth of the day and didn't want to admit she was almost surprised no bullets had come their way.

The interior door that led to the elevator required a tenant buzz them in. Luke pressed it. "Officer Luke Hathaway here to see Mr. Hernandez," he said in answer to the greeting.

The door clicked, and Luke pulled it open.

They rode the elevator to the twelfth floor and found apartment 12B. Luke knocked. Footsteps sounded, and the door opened.

"Carlos Hernandez?" Luke asked.

"Sí." Mr. Hernandez stood around six feet tall and had a dark complexion and kind eyes. His jet-black hair was neatly combed, and the pleasant scent of some kind of spicy soap wafted toward her.

Luke introduced them, and Carlos stepped back. "Come in," he said. His light accent held a warm welcome even as his brows dipped in concern. "I am so sorry to hear of the death of Chief Jameson. It's terrible."

"Thank you," Sophie said.

Once they were seated on the sofa under the window, Carlos settled into the recliner opposite them. "What can I do for you?"

"You work the 7 p.m. to 7 a.m. shift, right?" Luke asked.

"Yes, I work on any vehicles that need repairs for the next day."

"Did you see anything last night near the parkway?"

Carlos shook his head. "No, I was in the building all night like usual."

"What about when you went to pick up the truck this morning? The one that had been stolen?"

"No, nothing. I was told the truck was there and to go pick it up and examine it to make sure no damage had been done to it. I got there shortly before the police officers arrived and the keys were in the ignition. I checked the truck over and all seemed to be in order. Then the police started arriving, and I was told to leave the area. So, I did."

Sophie wanted to let out a huge sigh. She hated dead ends.

"But," Carlos said, "the worker who was driving the truck when it was stolen said he searched everywhere for it and couldn't find it. We watched the security footage and saw how the thief left but didn't see how the truck was returned to the property."

"We'll get those pulled and see if our technical analyst can find something. Anything else you can think of?"

"Nothing, I'm sorry. I'm not much help, am I?"

"It's not your fault," Sophie said. "Thank you for speaking with us."

"Of course."

Carlos saw them out of the apartment and they made their way to the elevator once more. Sophie pressed the down button and pointed to the Out of Order sign on the second elevator. "Was that there earlier?"

"I didn't notice."

"Me either." She sighed. And it really didn't matter. "Do you think we'll really find who killed Jordan?" Sophie asked softly. "Time is passing quickly. Just like the longer Jordan was missing, the less likely it was to find him alive. And we didn't. Now, the more time that passes and his killer isn't caught, the more likely it is that he won't be."

"Don't think like that, Sophie. You can't."

"Why? You are."

He cut his eyes at her. "I'm not sure I like that you can read me that well."

"I've had a couple of years to study you."

He raised a brow and shook his head.

"What?" she asked.

"I guess it's just becoming clear to me how closed-minded I can be. I judged you based strictly on your age, not on who you are. I don't really like learning that about myself."

She smiled. "But you're willing to change, right?"

"I'm willing."

The doors slid open and Luke placed his hand at the small of her back to guide her into the elevator. Bruno followed and sat next to Luke even while he nudged her hand for a scratch.

She obliged, thinking about Luke's confession. He'd judged her without knowing her. Well, at least she now knew why he never gave her a second look or bothered to talk about anything besides work.

Once they were on the way down, he got very quiet and seemed lost in thought. "I still look for my mother's killer."

Her breath caught. "What?"

"I was thinking about Jordan and the fact that his killer is out there somewhere. This is hitting home with me in a way no other case has, and it has to do with my mother's death. It's a long story. I'll tell you about it sometime, but for now, I need to concentrate on getting you back into the car without a sniper taking a shot at you."

His mother's killer? How had she not known about that?

Then again, their conversations for the past few years had been strictly professional and surface-level. Still. She would have thought she'd have heard something in regard to his mother's murder just by being in the office with everyone he worked with and was close to.

Or maybe it was a taboo topic, and everyone respected that.

So, she would, too. She wouldn't speak of it unless he brought it up.

The elevator jerked, and Sophie grabbed the rail to keep from falling to her knees. Luke slipped an arm around her and pulled her against his chest while Bruno barked and lowered himself to the floor.

A loud screech sounded, and the car raced down, then slammed to a stop. Only Luke's grip on her kept her from losing her balance. "What was that? What's going on?" she asked.

He grabbed the phone from the box on the wall and held it to his ear. Then let go of the handset. "It's not working. Try your cell."

Before she could pull the device from her pocket, the elevator jerked once more into a rapid descent. This time she clutched the rail and sank to the floor. Luke fell beside her, one arm wrapping her tight against him while he held on to the rail with the other.

"Luke!"

The car picked up speed.

Luke's hold tightened. "Hang on!"

Panic attacked her, and she dipped her head against his chest to pray. Then the free fall stopped, yanking the car hard. She slammed against Luke and he fell into the wall. Bruno barked and leaped on top of Luke.

"Why does it keep doing that?" she cried.

"I don't know," he said with a grunt as he moved the dog off of him with a comforting pat, "but the safety features are keeping it from plunging all the way to the ground—and keeping the car from going down as fast as it could—which is why we're not being tossed around like rag dolls. Regardless, we need to get out of here."

"Yes, getting out sounds really good," she said, heart thundering, fear choking her.

While he waited a few seconds as though trying to decide if they were going down again, Sophie dialed 911 with shaking fingers. Luke moved away from her to the doors, slid his fingers into the narrow opening and pulled. Nothing. "Stay on the floor and hold Bruno in case we fall again."

"911. What's your emergency?"

Sophie rattled off the situation.

"What are you going to do?" she whispered to Luke.

He looked up. "I need to find something to pry these doors open with."

Sophie turned her attention back to the dispatcher, who assured her someone was on the way.

The sudden pounding on those doors elicited a squeaky scream from her tight throat before she realized it was someone who might want to help. "We're in here!"

"I'm the building super," the deep bass voice called out. "We're going to get you out. Just hold tight."

"Hold tight," she muttered, but she did dig her fingers into the dog's fur. He licked her face and she settled her forehead against his, still holding the phone while the dispatcher continued to update her as to where the nearest police cruiser was.

The car dropped once more—the high-pitched squealing said the brakes and cables were trying hard to do their job, but something was working against them.

When they finally came to yet another abrupt halt, Luke scrambled to his knees and moved to the door. "Someone's at the control box, trying to override the safety features!"

Sophie stared at him. "You think someone's doing this on purpose?"

"You have a better explanation?"

"But how?"

"He followed us here, knew we'd be on the elevator and decided to take it out with us on it."

"Anyone could have been on it. How would they know when to try to send the car plummeting?"

"All he had to do was watch the floors. When the elevator was called to the twelfth floor after we'd been up there awhile, he figured it would be us going back down."

"But what if it wasn't?"

"Doesn't matter. It was."

"And he just happened to have an Out of Order sign to make sure we took the right elevator?"

Luke shrugged. "Maybe he saw it somewhere else and grabbed it."

A screech came from the doors. Sophie flinched and ducked, preparing for another drop. When it didn't come, she opened her eyes to see the doors slide open.

A pair of brown eyes stared down at them. "Are you two okay?" the man asked.

Luke grabbed Sophie's hand and Bruno's leash and helped them out of the car. Sophie sank to the floor, not even realizing she was crying.

"I think so," Luke said. "Thanks for coming to the rescue." Luke dropped beside her. "It's okay, Sophie."

"I'm Cliff, the super. She going to be all right?"

"Yes, thanks."

Sophie sniffed. "I'll decide if I'm going to be all right or not, thank you." She pressed her fingers against her eyes. "He could have killed us."

"I think that was the plan, but he wasn't counting on all of the safety features."

"I thought he was bold before," she said, dropping her hands from her face, "snatching me right out of the auditorium, but at least no one else was in danger. This could have seriously hurt someone else." She met his gaze. "You."

"Guy was in the elevator control room like you thought," Cliff said. "I had one of my workers try to grab him, but the guy fled. I called the cops."

"I called them, too."

His radio crackled, and he listened, then nodded. "Cops are on the way up."

Two uniformed officers arrived and Sophie rubbed her eyes. "He's not going to stop," she told Luke. "He's going to keep trying to get to me until he finally does."

Luke pulled her close. "No way, Sophie. That's not going to happen."

She took comfort in his words even while she wished she could believe them.

The next two hours passed in a blur for Sophie as she gave her statement and learned that a man dressed in a baseball cap and sunglasses had used a gun with a suppressor to shoot out the lock on the elevator control room door, then had done his best to sabotage the car. The only witness was a scared fourteen-year-old girl who saw him do it, then ran to her apartment to tell her mother. After a debate with her husband about whether or not to get involved, the mother had finally called the police.

"We'll get the description out," the young female officer said, "and see if anyone else comes forward. I wouldn't count on it, though. The fact that the mother did is a rare occurrence around here."

And then it was over. Sophie let Luke get her back into the SUV. As though he could sense her distress, Bruno put his head on her shoulder and she gave his ears another scratch.

Luke's mood had taken a turn for the silent and she figured he was probably processing the conversation they'd had with Carlos, not to mention the adventure in the elevator.

She shuddered and refused to think about that. She'd simply do her best to block the entire incident from her mind and if Luke didn't want to talk, she'd think about his previous words. The ones where he mentioned that his mother had been killed—and her killer had never been caught. It was a hard thing to digest, but she knew one thing. Luke was more determined than ever that another killer not go free.

Please, God, let us find the person responsible for Jordan's death.

Because she didn't know how his brothers and Katie would be able to move on without justice for the one they all loved.

TEN

The morning of Jordan's funeral dawned bright and sunny. Sophie would have thought nature was mocking their heavy hearts if she didn't know that Jordan would have chosen a day just like this for his final goodbye.

He'd been a cop and he'd had no problem facing the reality that every day could be his last, but he hadn't been morbid about it. Instead of scowling at the weather for its cheerful disposition, she thanked God for sending it. She chose to believe He'd done so in honor of Jordan.

The twenty-four-seven protection seemed to have staved off any more attacks and while she was grateful for it, it was driving her crazy, too. She wanted her life back. She wanted to wake up and realize everything was just a nightmare and Jordan wasn't really dead.

She sighed and pressed fingers to her eyes. She needed to stop wishing for the impossible and deal with reality, no matter how much she was struggling.

And then there was the fact that she couldn't dispel the guilt of taking over Sam's bedroom, but for the life of her, she couldn't figure out what to do about it. Sam had come home and taken the couch or used David's room when the other man was gone. Both men were gracious and welcoming, never making her feel like an interloper. Unfortunately, her situation was what it was for the time being.

"So, quit thinking about it," she said. But honestly, she'd rather think about that than what lay ahead.

The funeral.

Jordy's funeral.

She grabbed her phone and texted her dad. You and Trey okay?

Her phone buzzed, but it wasn't her father answering. Katie had texted. Sit with me today, please. With the family. If you're comfortable doing that.

Her poor, heartbroken friend. Sophie texted back. Of course. I'd be honored.

And she would be. While she styled her hair for the funeral, her mind tumbled back to that conversation with Luke as they'd left Carlos's home. Luke's mother had been murdered and he still hadn't told her how or when. She could do the digging on the story herself, but she wanted to hear it from him.

Over the last three days, he'd stayed busy while keeping her near. However, he'd seemed to pull away, distancing himself from her emotionally and she wasn't sure why. As a result, they'd had very little time to talk about anything not related to the case. Or Jordan's funeral.

He'd tell her when he was ready. Obviously, he wasn't there yet.

Her phone vibrated.

We're fine, Sophie. You just take care of yourself right now. Give my regards to the Jamesons and tell them I'm sorry I won't be able to be there. I can't get off of work.

They'll understand. It's okay. You need anything?

Nothing. Love you, hon.

You too, Dad.

Maybe her father wasn't as helpless as she'd thought.

A text from Trey. What kind of fabric softener do we use?

But Trey was. She answered him and he, too, expressed his sorrow for the Jameson family.

With one last push on a bobby pin that held her

hair in a bun, she started when a shadow outside the window caught her eye. The motion jerked her hair down, ruining the work she'd put into creating the professional bun.

Sheer curtains covered the windows, but the way the sun was shining, she could make out the silhouette of someone wearing a baseball cap standing just outside her bedroom.

She strode forward to the side of the window and threw aside the fabric. The person stumbled back, caught his balance and took off.

"Luke!"

Her cry brought him running. "What is it?"

"Someone was outside the window! He just ran off."

Luke whirled and headed for the front door. "Stay here."

Pressing a hand against her chest as though it would help calm her racing heart, Sophie peered out the window to see Luke step into her line of sight, weapon held in his right hand. She waited, watching him search the area, ready to leap out the window to offer whatever meager assistance she could if it appeared he needed it.

It didn't take him long to finish searching the yard. He even went out the back gate to check. Having him out of her line of sight didn't sit well with her, and she was on the verge of going after him when he stepped back into the yard and shut the gate behind him. He looked up and caught her eye. With a shake of his head, he walked toward the door.

Trembling, she checked the lock on the window, grateful to find it securely in place.

Several heart-thumping seconds passed before the sound of the front door opening sent her hurrying from the bedroom to find Luke tucking his weapon back into his holster. Bruno flopped onto the kitchen floor.

"Did you see him?" she asked.

"No. I saw his footprints, though."

Sophie pressed her palms to her eyes. "I think it was the same guy who kidnapped me from headquarters. It looked like the same ball cap."

"Okay, I guess this guy is back. He might have been watching the place trying to get you alone."

"But you're here."

"I went out the front door a little while ago to take Bruno for a quick walk just as David was leaving for work. I knew you would be all right. I didn't come back in the front. I took a shortcut through the back and came in that way."

"So anyone watching the house would have seen both of you leave," Sophie said, "not realizing you'd come back in, and thought I was here alone."

"Exactly."

"That's just awesome." Her tone clearly conveyed that it was anything but. "I'm going to go fix my hair again, then I'm going to need some coffee."

"I'm going to change out of these sweats and I'll meet you in the kitchen."

Fifteen minutes later, she returned to the kitchen to find Luke sitting at the table sipping coffee. Bruno lay stretched on his side, eyes at half-mast. At her entrance, his ears twitched, and his tail thumped once as though saying, "Welcome back." Then his eyes shut, and a light snore reached her.

Her gaze snagged Luke's and her breath stilled in her lungs. Dressed in his ceremonial blues, he was incredibly handsome. Although the days had passed in a blur of work, the evenings had been spent talking. About everything and nothing. Certainly not his mother's death. However, they *had* discovered a mutual love of Scrabble and chess, and so far were neck and neck on wins and losses.

And yet, even with the competition and light laughter as they played and teased one another, she couldn't help feeling like Luke was holding a piece of himself back. Like he felt like he had to keep her at arm's length. She didn't like it but wasn't sure what to do about it. Or if there even was anything she *could* do.

"Sophie?" Luke raised a brow.

"Sorry. I was just thinking." Ignoring the flush creeping into her cheeks, she grabbed a mug and placed the coffee pod into the maker and shut the lid.

"Are you okay?"

"As okay as I can be. I can't believe we'll bury our boss today. It's surreal."

"I know. Did you get some sleep at least?" he asked.

"Not really."

"Yeah."

The wealth of understanding in his voice vaporized all thoughts of her crazy attraction to the man and the fact that she knew he was attracted to her even though he was fighting it.

Today was about Jordy, not about what was possibly developing between her and Luke. "Katie texted me," she said. "She wants me to sit with the family."

"That doesn't surprise me. She thinks of you as a sister."

Sophie nodded. The tightness in her throat blocked any words she might have.

He stood and wrapped his arms around her, his lips next to her ear. "It's okay, Sophie."

"What is?" For the moment, his barriers were down and she closed her eyes, allowing herself to take comfort in his embrace.

"The fact that we want to smile. Or laugh. Don't feel guilty because you have flashes of joy."

His spot-on assessment of her feelings sent her emotions reeling. The fact that he was willing to go that deep into a conversation gave her hope. "My mind knows you're right. Maybe after the funeral—or after we find his killer—my heart will allow the smiles and laughter without the accompanying guilt."

"It'll come," he said, stepping back. "It may take a while, but it'll come."

"You speak from experience."

"Yes."

"Tell me." She'd vowed not to bring it up but felt compelled to do so.

He stared into his coffee as though he'd find the answer. Sophie stayed still, sensing if she moved, the moment would vanish.

"My mother was killed when I was eight years old," he finally said. "I know I mentioned it. I'm sorry I haven't explained sooner. The truth is I hate talking about it. Because with the telling and remembering, the grief and regret comes back."

"What happened?" she asked softly.

"A carjacking." His words, so quiet they barely reached her ears, held a wealth of emotion.

"Oh, Luke," she whispered. "I'm so sorry. How awful."

"I was at a martial arts class one evening. I was at the dojo five days a week for their after-school program and I loved it because I got to take karate, too. I saw Mom drive up on time like always, but I wasn't ready to leave yet because I had a belt test coming up the next day and wanted to go through the forms one more time. So, I pretended I didn't see her."

"What happened?"

"Halfway through my routine, a loud crack broke through my concentration. I spun to see a man in a ski mask pull my mother from the driver's seat and throw her to the asphalt." He pressed fingers to his eyes. "He got in the car and drove off, leaving my mother dying on the ground. He'd shot her in the head. She'd lowered her window because it was a beautiful fall evening, her favorite time of year. And he just walked up and shot her." He lowered his hand from his eyes and looked at her. "If I hadn't made her wait, if I had walked out of there on time, we would have left and she would still be alive."

"You were a kid, Luke," Sophie said, covering his hand with hers. "You can't shoulder that blame. That belongs to the man who killed her."

He offered her a small sad smile. "I know. Mentally, I do. I just…" He shook his head. "I've been thinking about her a lot since we found Jordan."

"Because her killer was never found?"

"Yeah." He stood and dumped the remainder of his coffee in the sink, then turned. "I can't let another killer get away, Sophie, I can't."

"We won't," she said, her words a promise. "We won't."

ELEVEN

Luke gave himself a mental shake. Once again, he'd spilled his guts about a topic he never talked about. And spilled them all over Sophie. A woman he was extremely attracted to and needed to keep his distance from. Emotionally, if not physically since he was determined to protect her. And yet, he couldn't seem to rein in his tongue. She was such a good, active listener that he could almost feel her compassion soothing his wounded childhood self. It was like he craved that.

Well, it had to stop. Period. "Are you ready? I don't want to be late." She flinched at his snapped words and he cleared his throat. "Sorry. I'm just… I didn't mean to be abrupt. I'm sorry."

Sophie stood. "It's okay, Luke. We're all on edge. Let's go."

With Bruno in his area and Sophie once again in the passenger seat, Luke started the vehicle and headed for the church. His eyes alternated between the road and the rearview mirror. The fact that someone had been at her window—and *knew* that it was hers—had his nerves on edge. Sophie's, too, apparently, as he caught her watching the mirrors, as well. Good. She needed to be on guard.

When they turned into the parking lot, it was already overflowing with cars parked anywhere they could find a spot. Police cars and SUVs lined one side of the lot and down the street and around the block. News helicopters cluttered the air, sharing space with the police choppers.

"I've been to more police funerals than I would like to remember, but I've never seen a turnout like this. Are there any officers left to guard the city?" she asked. Her wide eyes bounced from one area to the next.

He smiled. At least he hoped it was a smile. "Plenty." She knew it as well as he, but he had to admit that it looked like every officer in the state had come out to pay their respects to a man who had sparked admiration in each person he'd ever met or worked with.

"Do you think he's here?" she asked. "The person who killed him?"

Instant tension threaded across his shoulders and the base of his neck. "It's definitely possible."

"Have you heard anything more about what killed him? I know the toxicology report won't be back for a while, but it seems like there should be some kind of news."

"That was Elena on the phone earlier, calling to tell me her initial assessment that his death is somehow related to his heart was correct, but that's pretty much all she can tell us right now."

Sophie sighed. "I want answers, and I want them yesterday."

"We all do." She was stalling. Asking questions she already knew the answers to. He didn't blame her, but… "We have to go in, Sophie."

With her eyes on the front door of the large church, she gave a short nod. "I know."

"Sitting here dreading it isn't going to make it any easier."

"I know that, too."

"Then I'm going to pull as close as I can to the back door, let Bruno out, and come around and open your door. Once you're safely inside with some officer friends, I'll move the SUV and join you. Bruno can stay with you until I return and then we'll find Katie and the others."

"You think he would take a shot at me here?"

"I'm not putting anything past this guy."

She nodded. "Okay. Thanks. I'm ready."

Once she was inside, Luke parked and returned to find her right where he'd left her. With three other K-9 officers and Bruno standing guard. She sent him a small, tight smile when he stepped through the door, and he gave a nod of thanks to the other officers. Cupping her elbow, he escorted Sophie to the front row and seated her next to Katie.

Katie's gaze met his. "Thank you, Luke."

He hugged her. "I'm so sorry, Katie. I can't even tell you how sorry."

"You don't have to."

The brothers nodded, and six-year-old Ellie sat in Carter's lap, holding her father's hand and looking confused with the whole proceeding.

When Katie reached over to grasp Sophie's hand, Luke swallowed hard, clicked to Bruno and took his place, back against the wall so he had a good view of the room. He stood next to Gavin Sutherland and his K-9, Tommy. The dog glanced at him then settled his snout on his front paws.

"Hey, man," Gavin said. "Wondered if you were going to make it on time."

"Had to make a special delivery first."

"Sophie?"

"Yeah."

The music started, and they fell silent, but Luke's thoughts continued to swirl even as his eyes landed on the coffin at the front. Instantly, his throat went tight, and he noticed he wasn't the only officer in the room desperately fighting to keep his emotions under control.

Luke looked away, focused his mind elsewhere even as the soloist hit each note with a purity that sent chills down his spine.

Or were the chills from the fact that he couldn't be sure someone hadn't followed them to the church? Then again, someone wouldn't have to follow them. It wouldn't take a genius to figure out where they'd be. Where Sophie would be. But would someone really be brazen enough to try to attack her in the middle of a funeral with hundreds of cops around? Maybe. If he thought he could stay hidden—or escape in the midst of the chaos it would generate. Luke thought the last one might be the key.

He could see the back of Sophie's head from his stance against the wall. And if he could see it, so could everyone else. It just occurred to him that the balcony would be the perfect spot for a sniper to draw a bead on Sophie's carefully pinned bun.

Sophie held Katie's hand through the service, barely registering the songs or the message. Memories of Jordan spun through her mind like a movie reel set to the greatest hits. Fun times, his laughter, his love. So much love. For his job, his family, the people who worked for him, the dogs…and most of all, for Katie and his unborn child.

But second only to Katie and his family were his love of justice and his desire to right the wrongs perpetrated on others. Sophie ground her molars to keep her tears at bay.

Justice.

The word seared itself into her heart. "We'll get you justice, Jordan," she whispered. "We will."

Katie's hand squeezed hers, and Sophie realized she'd spoken the words aloud.

And then the church service was over. Now she had to make it through the graveside part without having a complete meltdown. But if Katie could do it, so could she.

The family stood and filed from the church. It was just a short drive to the cemetery and for a moment Sophie and the family were the only ones outside at the gravesite as they waited for the limos to pull around.

The hair on her neck prickled and she swept her gaze around the area before landing on the lone figure leaning against one of the large mausoleums. Sunglasses covered his eyes and he had a baseball cap pulled low.

She gasped and stumbled to a halt.

Katie stopped, too. "Are you okay?"

Sophie glanced at her friend, then back at the spot where she'd seen the man.

Only to find it empty.

"What is it?" Zach asked. Carter and Noah shot her concerned looks.

Chills danced over her skin in spite of the warm weather. "Nothing," she said slowly. "I'm okay. I just thought I saw the guy who'd kidnapped me over by the tree, but he's not there now."

"Someone we need to be watchful of or worried about?" Katie asked, her red-rimmed eyes narrowing.

"I'm not sure." Her friend had enough to worry about and the last thing she wanted to do was to take attention away from Jordan. Not today. She rubbed Katie's shoulder and shot Jordy's brothers a tense smile. "It's probably nothing but my recent paranoia. Please, let's keep going."

"No," Zach said, "we'll check it out. They won't start the service without us."

He and Carter took off to check out the area while Noah stood guard next to them.

The minutes stretched. Finally, Noah and Carter returned, mouths tight. Noah shook his head. "We didn't see any sign of anyone, but that doesn't mean he wasn't there."

"Let's keep going," Noah said. "Everyone's on the alert."

Katie nodded, and they all fell silent.

Ellie stepped up to her and slipped her small hand into Sophie's. "My uncle Jordy died, Ms. Sophie."

"I know, honey."

"He's in heaven. Daddy said he's with my mom."

Sophie could only nod, her throat tight. "Yes. I know he's in heaven. He loved God very much."

"I do, too. I'm going to heaven when I die."

"Well, hopefully, that won't be for a very long time."

And now, Sophie couldn't help wondering if she was putting the family in danger just by being at the service. She turned to Carter and gave him the little girl's hand. He raised a brow, but she shook her head.

The limos finally pulled to a stop next to them and Katie slid in the back seat. Sophie joined her. While the others' attention was diverted as they loaded into the vehicles, Sophie leaned over to her friend. "I think I should leave," she whispered.

"Leave? Why?"

"I don't want to put any of you in danger by being close to you. Someone is after me." She swallowed. "And I don't think he cares who he hurts. I also don't want to be the cause of any disruptions on this day."

Katie linked her arm through Sophie's. "You're not going anywhere." Her eyes narrowed. "If Jordan's killer is here, then he's going to see that we have you surrounded and he's going to have to go through us to get to you. He's not getting another one of us." She kept her voice low, but her vehemence came through loud and clear.

Insisting she leave would only cause Katie more distress so all Sophie could do was nod and squeeze her friend's hand. And then the limos were pulling up next to the two tents.

The first one held a K-9 SUV like the one Jordan had driven. Covered in roses, it was a stark reminder that her friend would never again climb behind the wheel. The second tent held several rows of chairs for the family. Jordan's casket had been wheeled front and center.

Sophie tightened her lips and darted frantic glances around the scene. Where was Luke? As part of Jordan's unit, he should be near the family during the next part of the service.

She stepped under the tent and sat in the end row seat so that Katie could sit next to her mother-in-law followed by Jordan's father and brothers. As soon as they were all seated, a soulful bagpipe solo started, the clear mournful notes of "Amazing Grace" lifting and sweeping around her, causing that ever-present tension in her throat to grow into a near-strangling lump.

Sophie lifted her gaze to the coffin directly in front of her and swallowed hard, hoping the knot would lessen while refusing to let the tears fall. She blinked and drew in a deep breath, needing her vision clear.

Surrounded by police officers, she should be able to focus on being there for Katie and getting through the day without a complete meltdown, but her nerves wouldn't settle. That feeling of being watched crept over her once more and she started studying faces, trying to catch the eyes of whoever seemed to be triggering the sensation. No one stood out and she shook her head, wondering if she truly was just being paranoid. Not that she didn't have reason to be.

And yet there was nothing she could see that should have her nerves gathered so tight. It was what she couldn't see that worried her.

When Jordan's family was seated, the others gathered around the tent, forming a protective circle around them just as the song faded to a doleful end.

The only sounds were the occasional cough, sniff or shuffle from those attending.

Once again, Sophie swept the crowd and easily found Luke about ten yards away in the line of blue. No blending in for him. Everything about him stood out to her. Sorrow and grief had etched his face into hard lines, but his chin jutted, and his shoulders never sagged. She drew comfort from his strength.

His gaze locked on hers and his brow rose as though asking her if she was all right. She gave a slight nod. He returned it.

The rest of the service passed in a blur only to come into sharp focus when everyone fell into an expectant hush.

Sophie's gut twisted. She wasn't ready for this part.

The final call.

Radio static sounded over the loudspeakers and

a sob slipped from Katie's lips. Sophie reached over to clasp her friend's hand as dispatch came on.

"Central to Officer 75990."

Silence. Waiting.

"Central to Officer 75990."

More silence. More waiting for the answer that would never come again.

"Chief Jordan Jameson, please respond."

Tears flowed freely now for Sophie. She simply couldn't control them. Katie's grip tightened.

"Chief Jameson," dispatch said, "no response. Officer 75990, Jordan Jameson, is end of watch. He has gone home for the final time."

A long, loud beep resembling that of a flatlining patient pierced the air. Gasping sobs came from all directions.

Then dispatch finished the End of Watch Call by saying, "Chief Jameson, the city of New York and the K-9 unit thank you for your service and your sacrifices. May you rest in peace with your eternal Savior. We will miss you."

Sophie thought the dispatcher may have smothered a sob on the last word.

More radio static. More muffled sounds of grief.

Then a heavy, misery-laden silence surrounded them, pressing in on her. Sophie likened it to suffocating. Could one actually die from grief? She drew in a deep breath and used the tissues she finally remembered she had to wipe her cheeks.

The bagpipes broke into the stillness once more and the strands of "It Is Well with My Soul" nearly undid her.

She couldn't do this. Jordy had been her friend, her boss, her support when she'd needed it. He'd given a green kid fresh out of college a chance because he said he saw great potential in her. He'd believed in her like her own father and it had left a permanent impression on her heart.

"I know he's with you, God, but we're going to miss him like crazy," she whispered so low not even Katie noticed.

Luke's gaze touched hers again and for a moment, it was just the two of them, drawn together by their shared sorrow, somehow finding strength in the visual connection.

When the song ended, Zach stood and walked toward the podium. His jaw like granite, he looked out over those who'd come to say goodbye to Jordan.

Sophie swallowed and glanced around, still on edge after seeing the man in front of the mausoleum.

"I have a lot of memories of Jordan," Zach said. "Good times, bad times, crazy times. Times we swore each other to secrecy over. But one memory that stands out the most is… Well, Jordy's the reason I'm a cop." His voice broke and he took a moment to gather his composure. "You see, I'm dyslexic, which means school was never fun for me, but I graduated high school and decided to go to the police academy. About halfway through it, I was ready to give up."

Sophie stared. Oh, how she could relate.

"But Jordy wouldn't let me." Zach cleared his throat again and drew in another steadying breath. "He helped me study, he figured out how to channel my attention by using short spurts of study time followed by some kind of exercise. Whether it was running with the dogs or going to get ice cream." A tear slipped down his cheek and dripped off his chin. He looked up. "Jordy was one of the most unselfish people I've ever met. Even as a kid, he always put others first."

Sophie's heart thudded even harder, beating in sympathy with the man whose struggles had been her own. No wonder she'd been so drawn to Jordan, looking up to him like she had her own father. He'd done for Zach what her dad had done for her—and she now understood why he never mentioned any mistakes she made in her scribbled notes. She clutched her tissue.

To her left, someone coughed. Then coughed again. Sophie saw the woman slip a cough drop into her mouth, then whisper something to the man next to her. She turned to leave, weaving her way toward the back.

The movement distracted Sophie, and she found her eyes drawn to another man in the crowd. She paused, letting her gaze linger. He reminded her of the man she'd seen near the mausoleum. The one who'd kidnapped her. But no, that couldn't be him. Could it? The man she'd seen had been wearing sunglasses and that hideous baseball cap.

This guy was wearing a navy blazer, but no ball cap even though he had on sunglasses—like so many of the men standing outside the tent in the direct sunlight. But for some reason she thought he watched her from a small opening in the mass of bodies. At first, she was unsure why she was so leery of him.

Until he turned his head slightly and she caught a glimpse of his profile. She sucked in a breath. It was the man from the podium. The man who'd been by the mausoleum—the same profile she'd stared at when she'd been in the passenger seat of his speeding car.

She swung her gaze back to Luke.

TWELVE

Luke frowned. Something was wrong. Sophie looked ready to burst from her seat. She slid her gaze from his to her left. Then back to him. Then to her left and back to him.

She was trying to tell him something. And it was urgent.

The next time she slid her eyes to the left, he followed her line of sight. And there was the man who'd kidnapped her from the auditorium. While the family sat, there was standing room only for the others—a wall of bodies surrounding the family. Luke didn't miss the symbolic gesture. Nor did he miss the fact that the man had started moving, slowly slipping through the spaces until he was about ten yards away from Sophie. And then he paused glancing at the podium, acting as though he belonged there.

Luke held still even though the man didn't notice him. What did the guy think he was going to do? Grab her with hundreds of officers around?

Or simply shoot her where she sat and run?

Impossible. He'd be caught immediately. Then what? The guy turned his gaze back to Sophie. Watching her. Waiting? For what?

For the right moment that he could reach her. For the break in the crowd that would allow him to act.

Luke nudged Finn. When the man leaned in, Luke said, "That's the guy who kidnapped Sophie the other day. I don't know what he's doing here, but it can't be good."

"Here?" Finn placed a hand on his weapon.

"I don't want to disrupt Jordan's funeral, but we may have to."

"See if you can get between him and Sophie," Gavin said. "I'll go behind him."

As one, they began to move, the dogs staying at their respective sides. They drew some notice as well as frowns, but Luke ignored them, his focus on the man whose attention hadn't swerved from Sophie. The service was coming to an end. Soon, people would begin milling, the crowd would pack in around the family—and Sophie. When would he make his move? Luke played out several possible scenarios even while he rushed to prevent it. Shoot her? Too obvious. Stab her? Quiet and easy but might not provide him with the ability to get away. Then what?

Sitting on the end of the front row, Sophie would be easier to get to than if she'd been in the middle. Or on the back row where the crowd offered a buffer against anyone approaching from the rear.

The need to reach her pushed him faster—which was like trying to hurry through quicksand. The crowd was thick but thankfully not packed tight. Still, it made rushing impossible. For a moment, he lost sight of the man. His attire allowed him to blend in easily.

"He lived well," Zach was saying from the podium. "He knew how to have fun and he knew when to be serious. He was a shining example for all of us who loved him and looked up to him. Despite what the newspapers are reporting, Jordan did not kill himself. He was murdered, and you'd better believe that my family will do whatever it takes to bring his killer to justice." Zach's grief-ravaged voice rose in his passion to convey his feelings about his brother.

*Amen*s echoed through the crowd and Zach nodded to the minister, who returned to the podium to start the closing prayer.

Luke listened with half an ear as he once more caught sight of the man stalking Sophie. Still far enough away, but closing in.

Then the service was over, and people stood. Luke maneuvered Bruno so he could slip between Sophie and the man who'd just now noticed him.

With a scowl, the guy froze, spun and started weaving back through the crowd. Luke gripped

Sophie's arm. "Stay with Katie and the family." Then he was on his radio, giving a description of the fleeing man. Officers immediately responded, but Luke had lost sight of him. He radioed in the last place he'd seen him even as he continued to follow in that general direction.

Finn closed in behind Luke. "There!" Luke caught a glimpse of a figure heading toward a line of vehicles at a fast jog. Something fell from his navy blue blazer just before he slipped around a massive mausoleum and disappeared. Other officers raced past Luke, who drew to a stop and knelt.

A syringe.

Meant for Sophie, no doubt. Well, that explained his attempt to get as close as possible. And he would have if she hadn't spotted him.

Gavin reached him. "What is it?"

"Do you have an evidence bag on you?"

"No. I'll get one." Gavin hurried off, his K-9, Tommy, loping along beside him.

Luke's radio crackled, and Finn's voice came through. "We lost him. He jumped onto the back of a motorcycle and sped off. We've got it called in and they're sending a chopper to look for him."

"Ten-four."

When Gavin returned with the bag and a pair of gloves, Luke collected the syringe, dropped it in the bag, then sealed it. He pulled a pen from his vest and labeled the bag.

"Was he wearing gloves?" Gavin asked.

"I don't know. I didn't get close enough to see." Luke met Gavin's eyes. "He was trying to get close enough to inject her. It's quiet, subtle. A quick sting. And she might not have realized what happened right away."

"Giving him time to slip away, blending in just like he did anyway."

"Yeah. At least Sophie was spared, though." A shudder ripped through him. Handing the bag to Gavin, he said, "I'm going to get back to Sophie. I don't think that guy will show himself again today, but I don't want to take a chance on being wrong."

Gavin glanced at the evidence bag. "Sure. I'll just get this sent off to the lab."

That reminded Luke he still hadn't heard if any prints had been found in Sophie's apartment. He made a mental note to check on that tomorrow and clicked to Bruno. "Heel, boy."

The dog rolled to his feet in an agile move and slipped up next to Luke's left side. When Luke returned to the tent, Katie and Sophie were wrapped in a hug. He stepped up beside them and Sophie's eyes met his, but her words were for Katie.

"You promise to call me if you need anything?"

"I promise. Now that Jordan's parents are here, I promise not to be so clingy."

"You're a far cry from clingy," Sophie told her

friend. "You know I don't mind helping or just sitting. Or whatever."

"I know," Katie said softly. "Thank you."

Carter approached, his eyes and nose red, but his jaw firm. "We're going to Griffin's," he told Luke. "In honor of Jordan. He'd insist on it."

Griffin's Diner was owned by Louis and Barbara Griffin. Since they served top-notch food and had a premium location near the K-9 Headquarters, it hadn't taken long for it to become *the* hangout for officers and their dogs. Thanks to the Griffins' love of all things law enforcement, they'd built a specific area called the Dog House. Officers could eat in that area with their K-9s without the restaurant being in any violation of health codes.

Luke nodded. "Sophie, that all right with you?"

"Sure. Carter's right. Jordan would insist."

"We'll meet you there."

When they all walked into Griffin's, Sophie noticed every eye in the place turned to them. "We'll be in the Dog House, Lou," Carter said, his voice rough.

"Violet'll be right out," Lou said. "Sorry I couldn't make it to the service."

"It's okay," Luke said, shaking the man's hand. "We understand. And so would Jordan."

"Yeah." The man's nose reddened and he turned

away. "Free burgers in the Dog House!" His holler carried to the back.

"Dog House burgers coming up!" The cook's
answer had Lou nodding.

"For Jordan," he told Luke.

Sophie cleared her throat and hurried to find
a seat before she burst into tears. Coming here
was a mistake. Jordan had loved this place, and
his presence practically bounced off the walls.
The Griffins had dedicated this room to fallen
NYPD officers—many of them K-9 handlers and
K-9s themselves. Bruno had been named for Alan
Brunowski, killed in the line of duty. The officer's picture hung on the wall opposite the chair
she slid into.

Luke seated himself next to her. "You okay?"
he asked softly.

"What was he doing there?" she asked, her
voice equally low. When Luke didn't answer right
away, she nudged him. "Luke?"

"He was up to no good, let's put it that way."

"He was coming back for me, I suppose?"

"Looks like it. You're the one who saw him at
the podium. He obviously thinks you can identify him."

"But you can, too."

"I'm not sure he realized that. Before now anyway. You can better believe I'll be watching my
back from now on, though."

"Good." She nodded and sighed. "Well, thank you for keeping me safe from him."

He sighed as Carter, Noah and Zach settled their dogs, then took their seats at a nearby table. Luke shot her a tight smile and squeezed her hands. "Let's forget about him for now. You're safe here."

She swallowed and picked up the menu she didn't need to look at. "You're not telling me everything." She paused. "Was he going to shoot me? Strangle me? What?"

"Inject you," Luke said. "He had a syringe and it fell out of his pocket when he was running away. We sent it off to the lab so, hopefully, we'll know something soon."

She flinched. Well, she'd asked. "Thank you. I want to know everything. At least the stuff that pertains to me. It's the only way I feel like I can be prepared for...whatever." Sophie held his gaze. "Promise me."

He gave a slow nod. "Okay."

"You two telling secrets?" Reed Branson asked. Reed was tall with dark brown hair and eyes. Part of the K-9 unit, he and his bloodhound partner, Jessie, like Finn and Abernathy, could track just about anything. Reed, Brianne, Tony, Finn and Gavin rounded out Luke and Sophie's table.

"No secrets," Luke answered. "Just discussing something that *pertains* to Sophie."

"Hi, everyone," a voice next to Sophie said. She

looked up to see Violet Griffin, daughter of Louis and Barb, standing behind her, notepad ready to take their drink order. The burgers would be free, but they'd pay for anything extra. Violet had her long curly brown hair pulled into a ponytail. Her dark eyes were cast slightly over her shoulder to rest on Zach, who was seated behind Sophie. "I'm so sorry about Jordan."

"Thanks, Violet," Luke said.

Violet's gaze continued to linger on Zach for a few more seconds before turning her attention back to them. "I'm really worried how his death is going to affect Zach," she said, keeping her voice low. "He and Jordan were really close."

"The Jamesons are strong people," Luke said. "They'll stick together and get through this as a family."

"Of course. Sorry. I guess it's really not my business." Her gaze slid back to Zach, then she bit her lip and shook her head. "So, what can I get everyone to drink?"

Sophie raised a brow but ordered a water with lemon without commenting.

Luke and the others gave their requests, then Luke tilted his head and asked, "How's the airport business?"

Violet's lips curved. "It's going well. There's never a dull moment and it keeps me on my toes, that's for sure."

"Oh, that's right," Sophie said. "I always just

see you in here. I forget that you work at the airport, too." Violet's full-time job as a ticket agent at the airport kept her busy. But when her hours allowed, she could be found helping at the restaurant.

Violet shrugged. "It pays the bills, but I can't seem to completely give up working here. I love the customers and Mom and Dad need the help. Plus, it helps pay for the night class I signed up for."

"Night classes, too?" Sophie said. "Wow, you're incredibly busy."

"I like it that way, I guess."

"Doesn't leave much time for a social life, does it?" Luke asked.

Once again, Violet's gaze slipped to Zach. "No, not much of one, but that's okay. Maybe one day things will change."

"Maybe."

"Hey, Sophie," Gavin said, "I heard about the dog coming from the Czech Republic. She's supposed to be getting here soon, isn't she?"

"Any day now." Sophie sighed. "She's a Labrador retriever, and her name is Stella. Jordan was instrumental in getting her here because of a favor he did for the prime minister when he and his family were visiting last summer."

"What kind of favor?" Brianne asked. "How'd I miss that?"

"Jordan kept it quiet, but the PM's daughter

went missing for a short time. She snuck away from her security detail. Jordan and Snapper tracked her down." She sighed. "I hate that he's not going to be here to see Stella arrive." The table fell silent and Sophie cleared her throat. "Sorry, I didn't mean to…" What could she say?

"No, it's okay," Luke said. "We're going to talk about Jordan and remember him. He'd want that. And Stella… Well, she's going to generate quite a bit of publicity for the department, so we definitely have to put our best foot forward."

"And make Jordan proud," Sophie said softly.

"Exactly."

"Brianne's going to be working with her." Sophie smiled at the woman. Brianne's big brown eyes gleamed with anticipation at the thought of the challenge. "I know you'll have her working right up there with the best of them in no time."

"That's the plan."

While Luke ate, he observed Sophie from the corner of his eye. She might be young, but she was strong. And pretty. And smart. And—

And nothing. As long as he was her protector, she was off-limits. Not to mention the fact that she was so much younger than he. Only that didn't seem to be such a big deal anymore. But it should, right?

"Everyone okay here?" Violet asked. She refilled glasses while she spoke. "Can I get anyone anything? Dessert?"

Groans answered her.

She laughed and left to wait on the next table— the one where Zach sat—and Finn pushed his silverware to the side. He leaned forward. "So."

Everyone looked at him. "So…what?" Luke asked.

"This might sound a bit crass to bring up now, but it needs to be addressed at some point. Who do you think will take Jordan's place?"

The table fell silent.

"I think that's a good question," Gavin said.

"Probably one of Jordan's brothers, I would think," Reed said. "Noah or Carter would do an excellent job. They both have been around awhile and have some seniority."

Gavin huffed a short laugh and shook his head.

"What?" Luke asked.

Sophie's gaze bounced from one to the other, landing on Gavin, who looked aggravated and hesitant to say anything all at the same time. "What is it, Gavin?" she asked.

"Nothing."

"Something," Brianne said. "What? You think you should get the job?"

Gavin shrugged, but his eyes narrowed. "If you're going by seniority, we all know that I have it."

Brianne gave a light snort. "You're just sore that Jordan beat you out for the position when you were both after it at the same time."

"Disappointed," Gavin said softly. "Not sore. There's a difference." His gaze connected with Brianne's for a moment and Sophie blinked.

Tony Knight slapped the table and they all jumped.

Sophie jerked her gaze from Gavin and Brianne and placed a hand over her heart. "Tony? You okay?"

"No. I'm not okay. Jordan's not buried an hour and you guys are quibbling over who's going to take his job. It's disrespectful...and distasteful." He lasered Gavin with a red-hot look. "Today, of all days, you can't give your ego a rest?"

Gavin sighed and shook his head. "It's not about ego, man, I just—"

"I don't think anyone meant to be disrespectful," Sophie interrupted. "Tony, I know you and Jordan were best friends and it's hard to think about him not being there in the office. Joining us here at Griffin's." She looked away and swallowed. "But the fact remains, his position will need to be filled. And quickly. As much as Jordan loved this unit and everyone in it, he would want us to think about it and make sure the unit is protected and nothing falls through the cracks."

"She's right," Luke said.

Murmured agreements swept around the table.

Tony sighed and raked a hand over his head. "You're right, Sophie, but first and foremost, I think we need to stay focused on finding Jordan's killer. Let the powers-that-be trouble themselves with a replacement while we keep our tunnel vision on this investigation."

More nods and agreeing.

Luke pulled his phone from his pocket. "I keep meaning to check on your apartment investigation and if they found any prints."

Finn frowned. "How are you doing, Sophie? We've been so focused on Jordan and Katie that I feel like we're neglecting your issues."

"You're not ignoring them at all," she said. "I'm not going to say I'm doing okay, but I'm doing as well as can be expected, I suppose." Her phone buzzed. A quick glance at the screen confirmed it was her father. "I need to answer this. Excuse me, please."

"Of course."

Sophie slipped away from the table and into the quieter area near the restrooms. "Hi, Dad."

"I'm just checking on you. How was the funeral?"

"About like what you would expect. Sad. Devastating. Hopeful in that we know we'll see him again in heaven one day."

"Yeah."

"How are things with you?" She could hear traffic in the background.

"I'm fine. Your brother called me a little while ago."

She stilled. "Okay."

"He's enlisted."

"He really did it?" So, he'd gone from buying fabric softener to enlisting in the Marines?

"Yes."

Sophie rubbed her eyes before remembering she had makeup on. She dropped her hand and let out a long, slow sigh. "Okay, well, I guess it's his life." Did those words really come out of her mouth?

"That's what he says." Her dad sounded as surprised as she felt, but she didn't have the energy to do anything about it. "But enough about him," her father said. "I want to know about you. Did anyone ever find who it was that called the house looking for you? And the person who broke into it?"

"Not yet. I think they tried to track the call, but whoever it was used a burner phone. As for whoever broke into the place, that's still being investigated. So far, they haven't found anything." She paused. "You haven't had any more trouble, have you? Something you're not telling me?" She frowned, concerned he was keeping something from her.

"Not a bit. I guess the police car on the house is an effective deterrent."

Either that or the person was keeping up with her and realized she wasn't going anywhere near her father or brother, so why bother with them?

"I'm glad."

"And no one is bothering you?"

"I'm fine." It wasn't an outright lie. Her dad didn't need to know about the man at the funeral or anything else. He'd just worry, and she didn't want to do anything to send his anxiety soaring or she'd find him camped out nearby. "I have plenty of protectors surrounding me. Even if someone wanted to try something, they'd have a very difficult time getting near me." Like the guy at the funeral.

"I can't tell you how relieved I am to hear that. All right, hon, I've got to go. Let's catch up a bit later."

"Do you still have some of those dinners I made in the freezer?"

"I do."

"And what about clothes? Do I need to have a friend come over and do a load?"

"I think I'm fine for now."

"All right, then, let me know when you start running low."

"Will do, honey."

"Okay, Dad. Bye. Love you."

"You, too."

She hung up and sighed and tried not to think about her brother's decision. Trey was a big boy. He was going to learn some things the hard way. But she'd pray for him. A lot.

When she returned to the table, Luke shot her a concerned look. "Everything okay?"

"Just my dad checking on me." She took a sip of her water.

"I got a call while you were on the phone. They didn't find any prints in your house."

"Of course not," she said.

"They did find a pair of gloves tossed in your trash can, though, which explains why he didn't have them on when he punched me. But no, there weren't any prints. And before you ask, they were cloth gloves, not latex or vinyl, so no prints on the inside either."

"Figures." She sighed. "I don't suppose it would be a good idea to return home at this point, would it?"

"You're kidding, right?" Luke asked.

She grimaced. "Pretty much."

"You've had it rough the last few days," Finn said. "First being kidnapped, being slammed in the car wreck, the threatening call to your dad, your home invasion and then the attempted attack at the funeral. It's obvious that this guy isn't giving up. I'd say you need to stay right where you are where you have trained eyes watching out for you."

Sophie nodded. "I know."

Finn looked at Luke. "And we need to be prepared for him to try again."

Luke could feel his tension rising to new levels as the conversation centered on protecting Sophie.

"We have to stay focused," Gavin said.

"Exactly, so, no arguing about who's taking Jordan's place," Tony said with a scowl in Gavin's direction. After a chorus of agreement, they fell silent to focus on their food—and thoughts.

"I said you're overdoing it and you don't need to be walking out to your car alone at night." Zach's voice came from behind him and Luke turned to see Violet standing next to Zach, hands on her hips.

"Well, I don't see how that's any of your business," she snapped. "I'm a big girl and can take care of myself."

"What's going on?" Luke asked.

Zach scowled. "She's taking a night class at the college and it's not safe."

"It's perfectly safe, Zach, I promise."

Zach's brows rose as he realized they were the center of attention in the small back room. He flushed. "So, are you taking precautions? Watching behind you? Making sure you're not being followed?"

"Come on, Zach, you're making too big a deal out of this. I have my pepper spray."

"Pepper spray! Don't you know someone can take that away from you and use it on you?"

Violet stamped a foot. "Do you really think I'm so stupid and careless? That I'm completely incompetent? Wow, you really don't think much of me at all, do you?"

"That's not what I—"

Violet spun and disappeared back into the kitchen.

Zach huffed and pinched the bridge of his nose while silence reigned for an uncomfortably long few seconds. Then he threw his napkin on the table as he stood. "Excuse me, folks, show's over. I'm going to grovel in private."

"That's the smartest thing you've said in the last fifteen minutes," Luke murmured.

Sophie turned wide eyes on him as Zach disappeared to find Violet. "What was that all about?"

"I have my suspicions," he said.

Twenty minutes later, Luke paid the bill for both him and Sophie, left a tip on the table and stood. "Are you ready?" he asked Sophie. Bruno stood when Luke did. The dog stretched and kept his eyes on Luke, who scratched his ears.

"More than," Sophie said. "I'm exhausted. I want to check on Katie, though."

"You want to go by the house?"

She hesitated. "No. She's got Jordan's parents there and Noah, Carter and Zach will be heading that way, too, so I think I'll just text her when we get in the car."

Together, they left the restaurant and stepped into the cool night air. "I love this time of year in New York," she said. "Not too hot, not too cold—and not too humid."

"All one day of it?" Luke said with a smile. "You realize tomorrow it could be thirty degrees."

She gave a soft laugh. "I know, so let me enjoy it while it lasts."

He held her arm as they started across the street, Bruno trotting on his left side, Sophie on his right. Halfway to the other side, a loud roar reached him and when he turned, a single headlight blinded him.

Without thinking, Luke tightened his grip and yanked Sophie away from the path of the motorcycle. Two gunshots rang out. Glass shattered behind them.

Sophie cried out and stumbled against him. Luke went to his knees in front of the car parked on the side of the street, pulling Sophie with him. His shoulder slammed into the bumper. Pain shot through him even as he rolled on top of her, shielding her.

The motorcycle zipped past so close Luke felt the heat of exhaust on his cheek. Bruno barked and bounded next to Luke. "It's okay, boy. Sophie, are you all right?" He rolled off her and ran his hands over her face. "He missed, right? You're not hit?"

"No. I'm…okay. What just happened?" Sophie croaked, clinging to him and trembling.

"Luke! Sophie! Are you two okay?" Zach yelled as he and the others tumbled out of the restaurant.

"Yeah, go after him." Luke pointed. "That way."

Finn's vehicle was closest. He and Abernathy hurried to jump in, then bolted after the disappearing motorcycle. The others soon followed after him while Luke ignored the throbbing in his knees and hauled them both to their feet. His mind raced. That could have been bad. Not that he wasn't grateful, but he almost couldn't believe the guy had missed.

"He shot at us," Sophie said. "He really did."

"Yes." He thought she might be in shock. He scanned the street, looking for anyone else who might have criminal motives on their mind. Bystanders pointed. Some held their cell phones. Others just rushed to get away from the scene. "Let's get you in the car while we wait to hear if the others managed to catch up with him."

"Did you get the plate?" she asked.

"No. Sorry. I was too busy trying to make sure you weren't hurt."

"And I appreciate it very much," she said.

He squeezed her hand and led her to the cruiser. Bruno hopped inside, and Luke helped Sophie get settled into the passenger seat. He took her hands in his and wondered if his pulse would ever slow down. "That scared me, Sophie."

Her eyes locked on his and his heart gave that funny little beat it often did whenever he was in her presence—and had a moment to acknowledge the attraction he had no business feeling.

So, knowing they were out of sight of any prying eyes thanks to the tinted windows, it made perfect sense for him to lean in and kiss her. With most of the others dealing with the motorcyclist or focused on documenting an accurate account of what had just happened, and with the danger abated for a moment, Luke was able to let his guard down a fraction and lose himself in the brief second of kissing Sophie.

And realized he might have just made a huge mistake. Not that kissing her was wrong. Quite the opposite. It felt right and good and perfectly natural. Only now, he'd never be able to go back to not kissing her. He lifted his head and gazed down at her.

She blinked, shock and bemusement stamped on her features.

"Ah, sorry," he said. "I probably shouldn't have done that." *Probably*, nothing. He *definitely* shouldn't have done that.

Her bemusement flipped into a frown. "Why not?"

"Because—" How did he explain? "Because I'm supposed to be protecting you, not—"

"Not what?"

"Not looking for romance." Okay, that wasn't helpful at all. "I mean I need to focus on this investigation and not let myself be distracted by the fact that—" He sighed and closed his eyes for a split second while he ordered his brain to start functioning. When he opened them, her face held no expression. "Can you help me out here?"

"I don't know if I want to. This is pretty entertaining."

He huffed a short laugh and, finally, she cracked a small smile. "I like you, Sophie," he said softly. "I just—"

She placed a finger on his lips. "I get it, Luke. It's okay."

With a sigh of relief that she'd let it go and didn't seem to be angry with him, he rounded the vehicle and slid into the driver's seat. He caught Bruno's gaze in the rearview mirror. Even the dog seemed to be chastising him for his bumbling awkwardness. He ignored the animal. His knees ached, and he'd have to toss his uniform pants in the trash, but at least they were still alive.

And Bruno was still staring at him.

Ducking his head and stifling a sigh, Luke cranked the vehicle and headed for home. Halfway there, the radio crackled to life and he grabbed it. "Did you get him?"

"No, he got away," Noah said. "By the time we

got the chopper in the air and to the right location, he'd ditched the bike and slipped into the subway."

Luke groaned. By the time they got the security footage from the cameras, the guy would be long gone.

Sophie kept to herself during the ride home. She'd acted like everything was fine and that she hadn't been deeply affected by the kiss, but the truth was, she had been.

Every so often, she'd feel Luke's glance rest on her as though he wanted to ask her what she was thinking but wasn't quite sure if he should.

He shouldn't.

Mostly because she wasn't sure exactly what her emotions were at the moment. Part exhilaration from the kiss. Part dejection from his apologies for it.

And part anger.

An apology for kissing her?

Seriously, that should be in the *Guys Guide to Girls* handbook somewhere. If a girl is agreeable to being kissed, don't kiss her, then say you're sorry, because it won't go over well.

Luke's interest in her—and subsequent kiss—on a normal day would have sent her over the moon with happiness—and anxiety. She'd noticed him from day one, but it had been obvious he hadn't had a shred of interest in her. Which had been fine. She wasn't in the market for a boyfriend anyway.

However, when Jordan had disappeared, it had thrown them together and had apparently given Luke a different perspective of her. One she was glad of but still not sure she wanted to pursue because of her duty to her father and brother. Then again, they seemed to be doing well enough on their own. Discounting Trey's enrollment in the Marines.

Maybe once they found Jordan's killer, she would be able to consider dating someone. Okay, not someone. Dating Luke.

But what if Jordan's killer was never found?

She couldn't stand that thought, but the fact was, not all murders were solved. Like Luke's mother's. What a heavy burden for a kid to grow up with. With a sigh, she rubbed her eyes and realized they were on Luke's street.

He stopped and let the engine idle as he turned to her. "Let me come around to open the door and then we'll hurry to get inside, okay? I'll have to move my vehicle once I know you're behind locked doors with Bruno at your side."

"Sure." He didn't say he was worried about a sniper. He didn't have to.

He opened her door and she and Bruno climbed out. Luke wrapped his arm around her shoulders and tucked her against him. He dwarfed her small stature. If someone wanted to shoot her, they'd have trouble finding an opening.

Her human shield.

Some of her hurt feelings and anger faded. Some.

Once inside his apartment, he released her. "Lock the door while I move the SUV, okay?"

"Okay."

He shut the door behind him. Bruno paced in front of it for the next ten minutes until Sophie let Luke back inside. He tossed his keys onto the small table. Bruno headed to his spot near the fireplace and flopped down with a sigh.

"I guess he's glad to be home," Sophie said.

"Always."

"And glad to have you back where he can see you." She bit her lip and fatigue swept over her. While she wanted to bring up the kiss, she didn't have the energy. Everything had been said anyway, apparently. "I'm going to my room. I'll see you in the morning."

"What about dinner later?"

"I'll pass. Thanks. Tomorrow's a full day back at work and I need to get things ready."

"Of course."

She headed toward the hallway.

"Sophie—"

She turned. "Not now, Luke. We'll talk later."

He frowned and nodded, and she slipped into the bedroom that had become her safe area.

Pacing and thinking for half an hour had done nothing except give her a little exercise she didn't need. When her phone buzzed, she snatched it from the nightstand and glanced at the screen. Her brother. "Hello?"

"Sophie?"

"Hey."

"How are you? Are you okay? Dad said some psycho was looking for you."

Sophie raised a brow. "Well, I'm not sure he's psycho." Maybe desperate? "But yes, I seem to have picked up a stalker. Stay on the alert, okay? I don't think he'll bother you or Dad, but be careful anyway."

"Who is he? *Where* is he? Tell me everything and don't leave any detail out. I'll find him and put a stop to it."

"Trey, I appreciate the protective brother thing, but the truth is, I'm surrounded by police officers. You don't have to worry about me."

"Dad's worried."

"I know. It's what he's good at." A lump formed in her throat and she pressed fingers to her suddenly burning eyes. "Look, I'm okay right now. Truly. I'd tell you if I wasn't. But I've got protection and people looking out for me. If something changes, I'll call you."

"Promise?"

"Yes."

He sighed. "Okay, as long as you're sure."

"I am." She paused. "Dad said you'd enlisted."

The line went silent.

"Trey?"

A sigh filtered to her. "I did."

"Why don't you sound happier?"

"Because while I really think it's what I'm supposed to do, I want your blessing. I need it, Sophie."

Oh. Wow. That really did show some maturity on his part, didn't it?

"Okay, Trey. Tell me why you think this is what you're supposed to do."

He huffed a short laugh. "I don't know why. Because I'm nineteen years old and a junior in college and I don't have a clue what I want to do with my life. Why keep spending money we don't have so that I can graduate with a degree I may not use?"

He kind of had a point.

"But the Marines? Why them?"

"They're cool."

"Trey…"

"Sophie…"

She groaned. "Ugh. Just keep me updated, will you? I care about you and love you and want to make sure I'm being a good big sister."

"You're a great big sister," her brother said, his voice soft. Reflective. "You've been more of a mom to me than the woman who gave birth to me. I'm blessed to have you. But it's time for me to…"

"What?"

"Grow up."

"Leaving college and joining the Marines is growing up?"

"Yeah, I think so."

Sophie couldn't deal with this right now. "You need your education, Trey. You'll lose your scholarships."

"I know, but I'll get the education I need while I'm in the service."

She swallowed. "Well, there is that."

He laughed. "I've got to go," he said. "We'll talk later. Love you, Sophie."

"Trey…"

"I'm hanging up now."

"Fine. I love you, too, but—"

"But what?"

"Don't hang up." He didn't, and she bit her lip, blinking back the rush of tears. "Trey?"

"Yeah?"

"If you think this is what you're supposed to do, then you have my blessing."

Silence.

"Really?" he finally croaked, his voice thick with his own tears.

"Really."

"Thanks, Sophie. I love you," he whispered.

"I love you, too."

She hung up with a heavy heart, feeling like her brother was making a huge mistake and she was helpless to stop him from doing it. But he was going to, so she could at least send him off with a lighter heart. She'd support him and love him. She could do that.

And she could do something else, too.

She pulled out her laptop and set it on Sam's desk. For the next four hours, she focused on catching up with emails and everything that being Jordan's administrative assistant entailed. Including fielding questions from the media—and being reminded that Stella, the Labrador from the Czech Republic, was arriving in the morning.

It would be hard going back into the office knowing Jordan wouldn't ever walk through the doors again. It would be more than hard, but her support system was there. All of the K-9 officers and the people she came into contact with on a daily basis. It would be good.

Maybe if she told herself that enough, she'd start to believe it.

She couldn't help pulling forth one niggling thought that wouldn't leave her alone.

Now that Jordan was gone, would the new chief want to bring in his own assistant? Or would he or she be willing to give Sophie a chance to prove she would do as good a job for him—or her—as she had for Jordan?

Then again, would she even live long enough for that?

If Luke and the others had anything to say

about it, she would. But a killer determined to silence her was still out there and Sophie's nerves were just about shot. Wondering about her job was the least of her worries. She just wanted to stay alive.

THIRTEEN

Luke expertly flipped the pancake in the pan and set it back on the burner. While the batter bubbled, he thought. About a lot. But mostly the fact that his mind hadn't shut off since sharing that kiss with Sophie. Which had made sleeping restless. He'd decided bringing it up at breakfast would just make things more awkward.

"Do you need any help?"

He turned to find the subject of his thoughts standing in the doorway dressed in her office attire. With her hair pulled back into a bun and her black-rimmed glasses perched on her nose, she looked…intimidating. Young but professional. Capable. Faint shadows under her eyes were the only indication that she might've had a sleepless night, as well.

"No, thanks," he said. "I've got this down to a science. Of some sort." He glanced again. "Do you really need those glasses? I only see you wear them for work."

A small smile pulled at her lips. "No. I just wear them in hopes that they make me look older." He held out a cup of coffee toward her and she took it. "However," she said, "I have to admit, sometimes I wonder if it just makes me look like I'm playing dress-up."

He laughed. He couldn't help it. "You look great. Very professional and put together. Like you could do anything you set your mind to."

A flush crept into her cheeks. "Thanks."

He cleared his throat. "I'll be ready shortly. Help yourself to the pancakes."

"I've lost count of how many times you've prepared meals for me. I need to pitch in for some grocery money or something."

"Don't worry about it. If I start heading into the red, I'll holler at you." He placed the last two pancakes on a plate and handed it to her. "Those are yours. I'm going to scope the area and be right back."

"I'll just scarf these down."

While she seated herself at the table, Luke slipped out the door and scanned the area. Nothing alarmed him. Which meant nothing other than he couldn't see the danger if it was present.

"What do you think, Bruno?" he said softly. "You think anyone's out there watching?"

Bruno's ears perked at his name, but he didn't seem to be particularly interested or unnerved about anything in the vicinity. After one more careful sweep, Luke returned to the kitchen to find Sophie washing the plate in the sink.

"You actually made those pancakes?" she asked.

"Yes. Why?"

"They were fabulous. What was in the mix?"

"Ah…you'll have to ask Sam's mom that one. I just know how to pour and flip."

"I should have guessed." Bruno walked over to her and nudged her leg. She scratched the dog's ears and he settled himself across her feet. She nodded. "He's a good dog."

"He is. And apparently, incredibly smart."

"Apparently?"

"It hasn't taken him long to figure out you'll rub his ears if he asks."

A smile curved her lips, then faded as she glanced at the door. "Everything okay out there?"

"As far as I can tell, and Bruno didn't have anything bad to say. I moved the car to the front so when you're ready, we're ready."

"Well, if Bruno says it's clear, I'm ready."

"All right, then. Just like last night, okay?"

"Sure."

Luke tucked her up against his side and escorted her to the door. He had to admit, he enjoyed having her right there next to him. He'd keep that thought to himself, as he'd already hurt her with his wishy-washiness. Until he figured out what he wanted, he owed it to her not to lead her on.

Not that he was intentionally doing that, but his behavior could definitely be interpreted that way.

"Luke? You okay?" she asked.

She'd buckled up and was waiting for him to shut the door. Fortunately, he was blocking any line of sight to her. "Yes. Sorry. Just thinking." He shut the door and rounded the SUV to climb behind the wheel.

"Thinking about what?"

"Just…the future," he said, "and what it may or may not hold."

"That's some deep thinking."

"Yeah. And I need to stop doing that or we're going to be late." He hated being late.

He'd been late, and his mother had died.

And they'd all been too late to save Jordan.

Clenching his jaw against the reminder, he glanced at Sophie. She was on the phone, scrolling through emails. Her laptop case rested against her leg. "You get anything done last night?"

She looked up from her phone. "Yes, actually."

"Anything I need to be brought up to date on?"

"Nothing I can think of. I was mostly making sure all of the files were organized so that someone else would be able to make sense out of them."

"What for?" He frowned.

"Just in case it's needed."

"Why would it be needed, Sophie? Are you thinking about quitting?"

She started. "No, not at all, but whoever takes

over Jordan's position may want to bring in his own administrative assistant."

"That's not going to happen."

She blinked and gave a small shrug. "That's optimistic—and certainly what I'm hoping for—but you and I both know how fast things can change when there's a turnover in a high-ranking position like Jordan's."

"Well, it's out of the question this time."

He was being obstinate and pigheaded about the topic, but it scared Luke to death that she could be right. "We've already lost Jordan," he said softly. "Losing you, too, would shatter the morale around headquarters." Not to mention his heart.

You're not going there, Hathaway, remember?

She peered at him out from under those impossibly long lashes and he cleared his throat. "Seriously, we need you. You're great at the job and you have something a lot of others in the position didn't have."

"What's that?"

"You care."

"Yeah," she said, "I do."

"So, you're staying." He said it like it was up to him, but he'd certainly be very vocal in his opinion if the topic came up.

"Okay." Her word said one thing, her tone said, "We'll see."

Just like before, he parked as close to the back

entrance to headquarters as he could and rushed Sophie into the building.

"I'll be at my desk if you need anything," she said.

"I'm just going to park and then I'll be in."

He waited until she was headed down the hallway before exiting and climbing back behind the wheel. Luke shook his head. "You've got to get it together, dude, or you're going to find yourself in serious trouble."

Sophie stepped from the hall into the spacious lobby area of the three-story building and found herself blocked from her office by a large crowd of officers—with the notable absence of the three Jameson brothers.

"What's going on?" she asked as she pushed her way through to the inner circle. Then came face-to-muzzle with a beautiful Labrador retriever.

Brianne Hayes knelt next to the dog. She looked up and grinned at Sophie. "It's Stella, our gift from the Czech Republic."

The yellow Labrador retriever seemed to be relishing all of the attention. Sophie scratched the animal's silky ears. "She's beautiful."

"And fat," Gavin said.

Sophie scowled. "Never call a woman fat." But he did have a point. Why on earth would the Czech Republic gift their department such an out-of-shape animal?

He frowned back at her. "She's not a woman, she's a dog."

"She's a living creature, and she has feelings," Brianne insisted. She narrowed her gaze on Gavin. "Be nice."

He shook his head and turned, but not before Sophie caught the smile playing at the corners of his lips. Good, they needed something to smile about.

Sophie ran her hand down the animal's neck, over her back and to her hip. On her third pass, she felt something shift under her palm. "What in the world?"

"What?" Bree asked.

Sophie returned her hand to Stella's side and felt the movement again. She laughed. "Well, I guess we know why she's fat."

Brianne blew a raspberry. "She's going to develop a complex if you people keep ragging her about her weight."

"Wait a minute," Finn said, stepping forward. "Are you saying what I think you're saying?"

"Yep," Sophie said. "This is one pregnant pup. She's going to be a mama. And soon, I believe."

"You're kidding," Bree laughed. "They sent us a pregnant dog? Who does that?"

"Someone who didn't realize she was pregnant?" Sophie shrugged. "Jordan handled this whole thing personally, so I wasn't really in the loop other than to know she was coming." She dropped to her knees and looked the dog in the eye. "She's gorgeous and with the right training will make a great officer, won't you, girl?"

As if in agreement, Stella swiped Sophie's face with her tongue just as Luke walked into the fray.

Sophie giggled and stood. "It doesn't matter," she said, drying her face with a tissue she snatched from the nearest table. "Let's get her checked by the vet and see what he says."

"I'll take her down there," Bree said.

Sophie caught Luke's eye and he had the weirdest look on his face. Not a bad look, but one she couldn't decipher. If she had to guess, she'd say shell-shocked.

She raised a brow and his cheeks pinkened just before he turned away. He wasn't immune to her, that much was clear, but it was also obvious he was determined to keep a barrier up for whatever reasons he deemed important. And finding out those reasons would have to wait. She had work to do.

Bree disappeared with Stella trotting along behind her and Sophie headed for her desk.

Only when she got to her office door, she had to stop and gather her emotions, bracing herself against the wave of grief that was going to hit her when she stepped over the threshold.

"You okay?" Luke asked from behind her.

"No." She hated that the word sounded shaky. Without turning, she continued to stare at the door to her office. It wasn't entering her office that had her so emotionally paralyzed, but Jordan's space was attached to hers and she was going to have to step into that area that would no longer belong to him and yet hold his presence in a gut-wrenching way. "And I think that's going to be my answer to that question over the next few months."

"I get it. Want Bruno and me to walk in with you?"

"Yes, please."

He slid a hand down her arm and grasped her fingers. His were as cold as hers. Maybe, in this moment, he needed her as much as she needed him.

Sophie walked into her office and noted the closed door straight ahead. "Should we treat it like ripping a Band-Aid off?" she asked. "Just go over there and open the door and…"

"Face it?"

"Yes," she whispered. Face the big empty space that Jordan had seemed to make small.

Sophie led the way to the door, hyperaware of Luke's hand around hers, tightening with each step. With a shaking hand, she gripped the knob, turned it—and pushed.

The door swung in on silent hinges, just like it always did. She drew in a deep breath and entered. Jordan's desk sat in the middle of the room. The detectives also working the case had searched it and found nothing. She could see they'd tried not to leave a mess, but files were out of place, Jordan's coffee cup was on the window sill instead of on his round Yankees coaster next to his computer.

Tears welled, and she shoved them back, pulling her hand from Luke's and instantly missing his touch even while her mind desperately tried to focus on the job. "I need to go through all of this and figure out which cases take priority, which officers to remind about court appearances—and which officers can take over Jordan's for now. No one's made a decision on an interim yet."

"They will soon. I'm sure the commissioner's working on it."

Another deep breath and she was able to approach his desk to gather the files he'd been working on before he'd disappeared. "I'll just take these with me for now."

Back in her office, she set the files on the desk and Luke hovered. Bruno sat at his side. She frowned. "Did you need something else?"

"I'm worried about you."

"Oh. Well, thank you?"

"No, I mean, I'm hesitant to leave you alone. I think you should consider going into hiding."

Wanting to discount the idea outright, she opened her mouth to do so, then snapped her lips together and decided the suggestion at least deserved her consideration. "Where would I go? Some kind of safe house?"

"Yes. Exactly."

"And who would be there with me? Officers assigned to watch out for me?"

"Of course."

Sophie pursed her lips. "I can see how that might be helpful at night, but look around you, Luke. I'm surrounded by police presence all day long. He's not going to try to get to me here."

Luke rubbed his chin and sighed. "Well…"

"I just don't think that would be a very good use of our department's resources. I'd rather use that money to hunt down bad guys. Like Jordan's killer."

He started to say something, but the buzzing of his phone cut him off. He looked at the device and straightened. "We've just been called into a meeting. I've got to go."

"Of course."

"Be careful and don't go anywhere alone. If this guy will show up to a police funeral with plans to kill you, I'm not so sure he won't try something here."

She swallowed. He was right. "Okay. I'll be sure to be extra careful."

He left, and she wondered if she shouldn't have been so quick to say no to a safe house.

Because if someone could get to Jordan, he would eventually get to her.

FOURTEEN

Two hours ago, the commissioner had called a meeting and Luke now settled into the chair nearest the door around the large conference table. Bruno lay on the floor at his feet and Luke checked his email as the others filed in, cops and K-9s. When Noah Jameson entered followed by Gavin and Finn, Luke straightened. He exchanged glances with Finn, who took the seat beside him.

"You know what's going on?" Finn asked.

"No one's told me anything," Luke said. "A little surprised to see Noah here so soon."

"Yeah."

Gavin sat on the other side of Finn, and Luke saw him scowl at the sight of Noah, who stood just inside the doorway, his K-9 Rottweiler, Scotty, seated obediently at his side. Gavin's jaw tightened, but he simply sat back and placed a hand on Tommy's head. The Springer spaniel looked up at Gavin with adoring eyes, then settled at Gavin's feet, placing his nose between his paws.

Once the team was seated around the table, leaving the end spot open, the deputy commissioner entered, followed by the commissioner, Luke sat up a bit straighter.

The commissioner stood at the head of the table and pressed his hands against the tabletop podium. "Thank you all for coming so quickly and on such short notice. I had a few things to say to you and this seemed the easiest way to get it done. And—" he paused "—I wanted it to be more personal."

With his forefinger, he pushed his glasses up the bridge of his nose and blew out a low breath. "First, I want to say I'm truly sorry at the loss of Chief Jordan Jameson. He was an outstanding officer and I considered him a friend. He will be missed by all who knew him."

Silence fell for a moment. Then the commissioner continued. "I know you all have been working overtime trying to figure out the connection to Chief Jameson and anyone who might have held a grudge against him. We have detectives also working alongside of you who are anxious to make sure Jordan's killer is brought to justice. I cannot express how badly I want this person caught."

He paused. "I know I don't have to express it. I know you feel the same. I want to say that I appreciate you keeping me updated and request that you continue to do so each step of the way. Now," he said, "my staff and I have been deliberating—some might even use the word *agonizing*—over who will step into the mighty big shoes Chief Jameson left behind."

Gavin shifted, and Luke caught his laser-like gaze. He gave a small shake of his head and Gavin's scowl deepened. The room held its collective breath while the commissioner glanced at the paper in front of him. Luke suspected he didn't need it but was simply gathering his thoughts.

"Each person we looked at held extensive qualifications for the job," the commissioner finally said, looking up and letting his gaze land on each person at the table. "You are all exceptional officers. In the end, we chose Noah Jameson as interim chief until a candidate is found to fill the position on a permanent basis. I know you all will treat him with the respect you offered his brother and I know that Interim Chief Noah Jameson will do an outstanding job. Thank you. That's all for now. Do good and be safe."

No one moved, no one breathed. The commissioner nodded and exited the room.

Noah stepped to the podium and cleared his throat. "I will admit that this came as a shock when the commissioner asked me to step in as interim. I wasn't looking to do so but feel like I can honor Jordan by carrying on where he left off." He sighed. "You guys know me. You know how I work and I know how you work. I trust each of you with my life and I know Jordan did, too. Let's continue to keep each other in the loop and do our jobs."

All heads nodded in agreement. Except, Luke noted, Gavin's. The man glared, and Luke suspected he was biting his tongue raw.

"Okay," Noah said. "That's all on that matter. Just a couple of things and we can get back out there." He opened the file folder in front of him. "Luke, do we know any more about the man who kidnapped Sophie from the auditorium?"

Luke stood. "Unfortunately, no. We just know that she found herself on his radar when she caught him in the auditorium looking through Jordan's notes and called him on his presence. As near as we can figure, he knew the schedule and the people involved in the graduation ceremony, got there early and slipped the suicide note into the folder. Of course, Sophie was there early, too, and things went downhill from there. One thing that's very clear is he wants Sophie dead and will go to great lengths, including taking risky chances, to make that happen. He's also slippery as an eel and knows how to blend in with his surroundings—including a funeral with hundreds of officers in attendance."

"Then you stay with her."

"I plan to."

"Good. Anyone else have anything that might

help us catch this guy before he can get close to her again?"

Gavin stood. "We've looked at the security footage from the restaurant to see if we could find any information that would lead us to the guy on the motorcycle, but so far we've come up empty. He was on camera, but he had a helmet on and there was no plate on the back of the motorcycle." Gavin dropped back into his seat and Luke couldn't read the man's expression.

"What about Snapper?" Noah asked. "Any word on him?"

Brianne stood this time. "I talked to the people in the lab just before heading over here to the meeting. They got the results back on the blood found in Jordan's SUV. It's animal blood. And while it wasn't much, it's possible that Jordan's killer killed Snapper and wrapped him in something to keep the seats…clean. Then hid his body better than he did Jordan's." She choked on the last few words, swallowed and quickly regained her composure. "Or, it could be that Snapper had a slight injury and simply left the blood behind."

"Thank you, Bree," Noah said, his voice rough. "I appreciate the update. Anyone else have anything?"

A knock on the door interrupted them and Sophie stepped inside to pass Noah a piece of paper. For a moment, her gaze locked on Luke's and the memory of their kiss blindsided him. He shot her a tight smile and looked away, but couldn't help wondering if it was at all possible to have a happy ending with Sophie. He'd admit to being halfway in love with her already. Halfway. Didn't mean he had to go head over heels. But if he didn't put some distance between them, he was going to. Their kiss had left him rattled and running a bit scared.

Part of him wanted to talk to her and get an idea of what she was feeling, yet at the same time, he wondered if he shouldn't run while he could.

Coward.

Maybe, but he had no doubt that Sophie had the power to break his heart and he didn't know how he would survive that a second time—especially if he had to see her on a daily basis.

When the door shut behind her, he ordered his heart to throw the walls back up.

At least until Jordan's killer was found. Then maybe he could revisit the idea of a relationship with Sophie.

Maybe.

The commissioner had just left, but everyone else was still in the conference room. Before stepping into the meeting, the commissioner had stopped by to inform her that Noah would be the interim. Sophie had approved his choice and he'd seemed pleased with her confirmation.

Sophie settled behind her desk once more to

grab the ringing phone. If it was another reporter calling—

"K-9 Headquarters, how may I help you?"

"He can't watch you forever." Click.

The voice belonged to the man who'd kidnapped her. She'd recognize it anywhere. Sophie closed her eyes and drew in a deep breath. She would not freak out, get upset or otherwise give him the pleasure of rattling her. Not that *he* would know it if she did, but *she* would.

It took her a few seconds to get her shaking under control, then she called a friend in dispatch and asked for a trace on the number. She could get Luke to do it but didn't want to interrupt the meeting.

"I'll see what I can find out," her friend said.

"Thanks. It's probably linked to a burner, but I have to try."

"Of course. Stay tuned."

As Sophie disconnected the call, she wondered if maybe she should consider that safe house after all. She'd talk about it with Luke on the ride home.

Luke.

And that kiss.

Whew.

Thinking about that was one way to get her mind off the fact that someone wanted her dead and had just threatened her.

A shudder ripped through her and she pushed back from the desk to stand. And pace. And think.

Until Finn entered the room. "Sophie? You okay?"

"I'm fine."

"You're a lousy liar."

She huffed a low laugh. "Thanks." She waved a hand and told him about the caller.

His brows dipped. "That's not good. Have you told Luke?"

"Not yet. I think he's still in the meeting."

"He was finished when we were."

"Oh. Well, maybe he's working on something or talking to someone and will be out in a bit."

"Probably."

Or was he avoiding her for some reason?

Surely not. Finn and Abernathy disappeared down the hall and she returned to her desk to lose herself in emails and sorting files for Noah, making notes about each one. She and he would have to sit down together, and she'd walk him through the cases, as well as the duties Jordan had assigned to her. He could decide if he wanted her to continue doing her usual or change them up. Either way, she felt better about her job security. For the time being anyway.

When her phone rang, she stretched the cramp in her neck and checked the number before answering. Her tension eased slightly when she saw that it was her friend in the dispatch office calling back. "Hi, Carol."

"Sophie, I checked the number and you were right. It was from a burner phone. There's no way to trace it exactly, but according to the towers, I can put it about five miles from you. I sent a cruiser out to the area to see if they could spot anyone fitting the description of your kidnapper, but I doubt he stuck around long after making the call. He knows we're looking for him."

"Okay, thank you." She hung up and dropped her head into her hands. When would this end? With a sigh, she went back to her notes and forced herself to concentrate.

The next time she looked up, Luke and Bruno were standing in the doorway watching her. She blinked at the frown on Luke's face. "What is it?"

"You didn't tell me you got a threatening phone call."

"Finn?"

"Yeah, he texted me and told me to check on you and make sure you didn't go anywhere alone."

She shrugged. "I was planning to tell you when I saw you."

"Did you recognize his voice?"

"Yes. It was the same guy."

Anger flashed in his eyes for a brief moment. "I'm going to stop this person if it's the last thing I do."

"How?"

"I don't know. I haven't figured that out yet. Let's see if we can come up with a plan on the way back to my place. Are you done for the day?"

"I could work another forty hours and not be

done." She closed her laptop. "But I'm starving, and my eyes are burning. It's already past six so I'm ready to call it a day."

"I'll feed you," he said. "What do you want?"

The words were Luke, but the standoffish expression wasn't one he'd ever used with her before. She bit her lip, considering his features, and decided that if he was going to do his best to put distance between them, he would have to work through whatever was bugging him.

Probably that kiss.

Then again, maybe it hadn't affected him like it had her if he could so easily alter his behavior and treat her so coolly. Or maybe he was waiting on her to bring up the topic. But why should she? He was the one who'd kissed her and apologized.

Since they were alone, she started to say something about the kiss and stopped. He looked worn out. Maybe his demeanor had nothing to do with her. Maybe she was giving herself too much credit. Whatever the case, compassion stirred, and she decided to drop it. "It was a tough day, wasn't it?"

"Yeah."

She nodded. She was being selfish. They were all grieving and she was obsessing about a kiss. Later, after some time had passed, she'd bring it up. Maybe. If he regretted it, did she really want to know about it? Open herself up to the humiliation that would bring?

That was a big fat *no*.

She needed to let it go. For now.

And hope Luke would bring it up.

As strange as it may be, she had to admit that whenever she was with Luke, she felt safe. His determination to protect her allowed that. In spite of the person who seemed just as determined to kill her. She grabbed her purse. "Luke, can we talk about—?"

"Luke?"

Sophie turned to see Tony waving at Luke.

"Sorry to interrupt," Tony said, "but could I have a word? I can see you're ready to leave, but this can't wait."

"Sure." To Sophie, Luke asked, "You mind waiting?"

"Of course not."

He shot her a swift smile, then joined Tony in the small office off the hallway. The room was mostly used for storage—and private conversations. "What is it?"

Tony paced from one end of the area to the other—as much as he could pace with all the boxes stacked around the perimeter. "Reed and I were talking."

"About?"

"Gavin."

Luke leaned against one of the larger boxes and crossed his arms. "Again, about?"

"About…" Tony raked a hand over his head.

"Look, I know Noah's the new chief, but I'd rather not bring him into this. Yet."

"Into what? Something's bothering you in a big way. Spill it."

"What if it was Gavin?" Tony asked, his gaze not quite meeting Luke's.

"What if...what was Gavin?" Luke didn't like where the question was taking the conversation.

Tony sighed. "What if Gavin killed Jordan because he was still mad about Jordan beating him out for the position two years ago? What if his anger has just been growing ever since and he finally snapped? There. I said it. I should be kicked off the team for even thinking it, right?"

"No," Luke said softly. "I have to admit it crossed my mind, as well."

Tony froze for a second, then finally lifted his gaze to meet Luke's. "Really?"

"Yeah. For a brief moment, I wondered. Then felt like you. I can't believe that would even cross my mind."

"Oh man." Tony sighed. "I'm so glad you said that."

"Have you discussed this with anyone else besides Reed?"

"No. Neither one of us likes thinking it, much less discussing it, but I think..."

"What?"

"We should at least investigate and make sure he has an alibi."

Luke palmed his eyes and drew his hands down his face. He gave a slow nod. "Okay. I think that's a valid argument considering their history, but I'm going to go on record in saying that I don't believe it."

"Then let's prove it so we can defend him if it comes up with whoever winds up taking Jordan's place."

"Good idea."

"I'll get the ball rolling on that. You want to discuss this with him? He's going to be hurt and angry that we feel we even have to do this."

Luke shut his eyes and nodded. "Fine. I'll talk to him." He and Gavin seemed to have the least amount of conflict. He'd never been close to Gavin but had never had anything against the man except his attitude when it came to Jordan and his ambition. "Is he still here?"

"Yeah, I think he headed to his desk."

Tony left, and Luke joined Sophie at her desk once more.

"Everything all right?"

"Just some things I need to think about with the investigation. I have one more thing I have to take care of, then we can head out, okay?"

"Sure."

Luke left her and went in search of Gavin. He found him sitting at his desk, head in his hands. The big man looked defeated, his dark brown hair in need of a trim, his broad shoulders slumped. For a moment, Luke simply stared at the man, wondering if he was doing the right thing by bringing up the topic. He turned to leave, then stopped. No, it was probably better coming from him, because if he didn't ask, Tony would—and that would be a recipe for disaster for the whole team.

"Gavin, you got a minute?"

Gavin dropped his hands and turned. "Sure. Have a seat."

Luke settled himself in the chair next to the desk facing Gavin, and Bruno stretched out on the floor next to Luke. Gavin's dog, Tommy, shifted and crept closer to his handler, eyes on Bruno. "I need to ask you something," Luke said, "and since there's no right way to ask, I'm just going to spit it out."

With a frown, Gavin nodded.

"Do you have an alibi for the day and time Jordan went missing?"

Gavin didn't move. His eyes never left Luke's, allowing Luke to see the change as they went from friendly to frosty. "Why do I need an alibi?"

"Because it's been brought up that you and Jordan's rivalry may have escalated, and it would be a good thing for you to have it on record that you provided an alibi. Should it be questioned by anyone."

"Sounds like it's already been questioned."

"Not so much that anyone believes you had anything to do with Jordan's death, but out of the desire to protect you and have an answer if we're questioned about it."

"Questioned by whom?" Gavin flicked a glance at the others gathered near Sophie's office. "My unit members? Men and women I trust every day? People I'd die for? Them?"

"No," Luke said. "People who don't know you like we do." The statement stopped him. His own words echoed around him and he clasped his hands together as he leaned forward. "I don't think you had anything to do with Jordan's death. Not one thing. But it's well-known that you two went head-to-head occasionally and that he got a promotion that you were hoping for. For some people that would be enough to hang you right there. We want to be able to refute any such claims."

Gavin drew in a deep breath and then let it out slowly as though trying to decide whether to continue being offended or cooperate. Finally, he nodded. "I moonlight upon occasion, doing security for various events around the city." He held up a hand at Luke's start. "Only when I'm off duty and the people I work for know that I may have to bolt at a very inconvenient time. But usually, that doesn't happen. The morning of graduation, I was working a private event. Jordan had approved it."

"He gave you permission to miss the ceremony?"

"Yes. So, when you called to let me know Jordan was missing, I explained the situation to the client, then Tommy and I headed home to pick up the SUV before coming to help look for Jordan."

"Where was the event?"

"In Manhattan."

"So, your client can vouch for you?"

"Sure. And I think my neighbor could verify when I got home. But I drove my car so all you have to do is check the mileage and the GPS. I put the address in so I didn't waste time looking for it. The client also covered my parking expenses so there'd be a record of that, as well. No doubt I'm on the garage's security footage, as well, when I entered and left."

"Thanks, Gavin. I didn't want to ask, but at least we can tell anyone who brings up the subject why you're not considered a suspect."

Gavin shot him a sad smile. "But I was, even if for a short time, if you feel like you need to ask for an alibi."

"Yeah, I know. And we'll talk to your client, so leave his name and number, will you? But as far as I'm concerned, you're good."

"Thanks, man."

"Absolutely." Luke drew in a deep breath. "And now, I'm going home."

"Not without Sophie, I gather."

"No, not without Sophie." He slipped out of Gavin's cubicle and made his way to Sophie's desk, where she had packed up her bag and laptop and whatever else she needed. She stood at the window, looking out.

"You ready?"

She jerked like he'd pulled her from deep thoughts but turned and shot him a smile. "Sure."

Once they were seated in the car, Luke could feel Sophie's gaze on him. He could tell she wanted to talk about what happened between them. Specifically, the kiss. And quite frankly, even though he'd apologized and given her an explanation for why they should keep some distance between them, he was looking forward to kissing her again. Which unsettled him even further.

Completely put out with himself and his uncharacteristic behavior, he decided that instead of putting distance between them, they needed to have a heart-to-heart. If he could work up the guts to do it. First, he kissed her, then he apologized—and now he wanted to straighten things out.

Poor Sophie. She didn't deserve his indecisiveness. Although, to be truthful, if he wasn't dealing with Jordan's death and being so involved in the case, then the whole situation would be different.

He slid another glance at her. She was deep in thought, as well. He almost asked her what she was thinking about, but they were close to his apartment. His empty apartment. Sam and David were both gone. Sam out of town and David working until the wee hours of the morning. There would be plenty of time to talk.

A final glance in the mirrors reassured him that no one had followed them. Then again, whoever was after Sophie wouldn't have to follow. "Has your dad mentioned any more trouble at the house?" Luke asked. "The guys watching the building haven't reported any, but maybe he said something to you?"

Small talk. Nice job, Hathaway.

"No, no trouble," she said, her gaze still averted.

"Good."

Could he be any more awkward? Probably, so he fell silent and pulled next to the curb. "Gavin's on his way to take a shift on watching the house. He should be here shortly. I'll walk you to the door and then go park the car."

"Okay."

"Stay put and I'll come around and get you."

"I know the drill." And she didn't sound particularly thrilled about it.

Clamping his lips on a sigh and an apology, he made his way to her door and tucked her into his side.

As he hurried her toward the front door, he knew he was lost. She was small, but she felt just right next to him—like she belonged there and he hadn't known what he was missing until he found it.

The fact that he got her safely inside almost surprised him. "I'll be back, and then we'll talk, okay?"

Sophie raised a brow, then nodded. "I'm going to get a water. Do you want one?"

"Sure."

That she was speaking to him settled his anxiety a bit as he went to search for a parking space. After finding a spot, he came back inside and opened the back door to let Bruno out into the fenced yard. The German shepherd darted out and Luke headed to the den, searching for the right words—and not finding them.

When Sophie joined him, she handed him the bottle of water and took a seat in the recliner, curling her legs beneath her.

Glad to have something to do with his hands, Luke opened the bottle and took a long swig before settling on the sofa opposite her. "Sophie, I…"

She lifted her gaze and he swallowed.

"Just say it, Luke."

She wasn't going to make it easy for him. But then, why should she?

He sighed. "I wanted to say I'm sorry."

"You've already apologized for kissing me. It's not necessary to do it again."

"What? No!" He cleared his throat. "No, that's not what I was apologizing for."

"Then what?"

"For being a wimp."

She laughed. Actually *laughed*. "Luke, you're not a wimp. And I can't stay mad at you. I've been thinking, and it's been such a crazy time for everyone that maybe we're all acting a bit out of character."

"You?"

"Of course. I'm jumping at shadows, avoiding confrontations and conflict—"

"Wait, you are?"

Another laugh, this one self-deprecating. "Yes. My brother dropped out of college to go into the military and you know what I did?"

"What?"

"Nothing."

He blinked. "What do you mean, nothing?"

"Exactly that. I did *nothing*. I've been so consumed with the kidnapping, Jordan's death, Katie's mental state..." She waved a hand. "Everything. That I completely let it go. I let my brother make a stupid decision and I said nothing."

"Why is it stupid?"

She sighed. "I don't know that it is, to be honest, but I wish he would have at least finished college before enlisting."

"Can't he finish while he serves? Or after? Then it's free."

"I suppose." She pressed fingers to her eyes before dropping her hands. "And, he's nineteen. It's not like he has to listen to me anymore anyway. Not that he ever did." She shrugged. "But maybe I don't know as much as I think I do. Maybe this is the best thing for him. Maybe he does know more than I did when I was nineteen." She paused. "Regardless, what I'm getting at is that it's okay to be a little off your game right now."

"No, it's not, because if I'm off my game, someone—"

Bruno's sudden and intense barking yanked Luke to his feet. "Stay here." He pulled his weapon and headed for the back door.

"Luke, be careful!"

He paused and looked back at Sophie then the locked door. "Don't open the door to anyone but Gavin, okay?"

"Of course."

He hesitated a fraction of a second more before Bruno's second round of frantic barks sent him out the door.

Once outside, Luke hurried to Bruno, who paced the length of the back fence. His barking had ceased, but his hackles still bristled. "What is it, boy?"

Bruno whined and trotted over to Luke, who scratched his ears. Bruno might not be trained to take down criminals, but he was an excellent watchdog and very protective of his territory. With his weapon held ready, Luke called for backup and headed for the gate.

FIFTEEN

Sophie paced while she waited for Luke and Bruno to return. She checked and rechecked the locks, made sure all of the windows were securely latched—and paced some more.

What if Luke found something? What if something found *him*? What if he was in trouble? Should she go out and check on him?

But he'd said to stay put.

But if he was in trouble, she needed to do something.

But Gavin was almost there and would help.

But what if Gavin was too late?

Pressing her fingers to her temples, she prayed for wisdom.

The doorbell rang, and she left Luke's apartment to go to the building's front door. She stopped to check the peephole. "Gavin?"

No one answered, and she couldn't see anyone through the peephole. Frowning, she glanced at Luke's apartment. Should she call for Luke?

A loud thud against the door sent her reeling back. Another thud, then the crash and bang of the door slamming against the wall ripped a scream from her throat.

The man from the auditorium, the funeral, the one who'd kidnapped her, never stopped moving. His bloodshot eyes locked on hers as he stepped over the fallen door and bolted toward her, weapon aimed at her.

Shock at the brazen invasion held her frozen for a split second before she screamed again and turned to run. A bullet cracked into the wall beside her head and she threw herself to the floor with a jarring thud.

"Police! Freeze!" Luke stood just inside the back door, his gun aimed at the intruder.

A hard hand clamped down on her wrist and held the weapon to her head. "Back off!"

Luke's eyes never wavered, but Sophie could see her fear reflected back at her in the dark depths. "Let her go," Luke said. "You don't want to do this."

Her captor yanked her to her feet and toward the open door, keeping her between himself and Luke, using her as a shield.

"Luke!" Sophie shuddered, unable to gain any traction on the hardwood floor as the man dragged her backward. The gun moved from her neck and aimed at Luke. The tension in the man's body shouted at her. He was going to kill Luke.

"No!" She pushed his arm as he squeezed the trigger. The bullet slammed into the ceiling.

Luke dove into the kitchen, taking refuge behind the wall. Sirens sounded. Or was that the ringing in her ears from the gunshot?

Again, the man didn't hesitate. He pulled her out of the house toward his vehicle parked on the sidewalk. The engine was running. Sophie noted the neighbors coming out of their homes to watch and point.

She struggled against his hold, but like before, he was strong and angry and once again, she found herself in the passenger seat of his car. She reached for the handle and he grabbed her by the hair, jamming the gun against her neck.

"Don't, or I'll end this here."

Blue lights flashed in the distance and Luke appeared in the doorway, his gun aimed at the vehicle. But, of course, he wouldn't shoot for fear of hitting her. "You can't kill me," she said. "You need me to get away."

"Then don't try anything and I'll let you live a few more minutes." He removed the gun from her and threw the car into gear.

"Why are you doing this?" she cried as he peeled away from the curb. She noted his shaking hands, bloodshot eyes and scruffy appearance. He was on something. Alcohol? Drugs? Did she even want to know? "Please. At least tell me why!"

"You were just in the wrong place at the wrong

time." He glanced in the rearview mirror and tightened his grip on the wheel. "I've got to shake the cops." He shot her a glare. "You've messed everything up."

"Me? How?"

"It was just supposed to be a quick little job. Slip the letter in the envelope and get out. But no. You had to show up. Why couldn't you just mind your own business?"

Sophie's jaw dropped. Mind *her* business? She snapped her lips together and fought to think past the fear. He was going to kill her if she didn't escape. However, the longer he thought she would be useful as a hostage, the longer she'd have to figure out a way to escape. "What's your name?" she asked as he wheeled onto the highway. Flashing lights stayed behind them.

"Claude."

"Claude what?"

"Jenks! What's it matter to you?"

"Maybe I want to know the name of my murderer."

"I'm no killer," he said.

She let that one go. "You killed Jordan. He left behind a wife and unborn child. Why would you kill him and try to make it look like a suicide? Why?"

He let out a huff of a laugh. "I didn't kill that guy. I just told you I'm no killer."

"And yet you just said you're going to kill me."

She was trying to reason with a man in an altered mental state. Add in his desperation not to get caught and it was a formula for disaster—or death. There wasn't going to be any reasoning with him. If she wanted to live, she had to get away. Period.

Once again, he shot her a dark look. "I told you, I was just supposed to slip the envelope into the folder. It was easy money. No one was supposed to get hurt. But you…you messed it up and I'm not going to go back to jail."

Back? She swallowed. "And no one has to," she said. "If you didn't kill Jordan, then you can end this before it goes any further."

He slammed on brakes and skidded across three lanes of traffic, narrowly avoiding colliding with several vehicles. Horns blared, brakes squealed and Sophie gripped the door handle in order to keep from being tossed all over the front seat. The seat belt dug into her as he got on the expressway, then the next left, then a right.

Soon, Sophie lost track of all the twists and turns. And when she looked behind her, there was no sign of blue lights. "Come on, Claude. You can go to the police station and turn yourself in. I'll tell them you didn't hurt me and you were the perfect gentleman. You won't get off scot-free, but they'll probably give you a break."

He scoffed. "I've never caught a break a day in my life."

"Maybe that can change if you do the right thing."

"And besides," he said as though she hadn't spoken, "I'm connected to a cop killer. They'll never believe anything I say."

"You know who killed Jordan?"

He glanced at her, then back at the road.

"Come on, Claude, tell me, please. Why did he want Jordan dead?"

"Because he—" He bit off the words and yanked the wheel once more.

Darkness was approaching, but she caught sight of the water straight ahead. Which body of water? She wasn't familiar with this part of Queens and her heart pulsed with dread and terror. "Because he what, Claude?"

"Enough! It doesn't matter! As soon as you're dead, I'm a free man."

"If you kill me, you'll never be free."

"Shut up, shut up, shut up!" He threw the car in Park and grabbed his weapon, bringing it up to her face.

"What are you doing?"

"I don't want to kill you, but I don't have a choice. I can't go back to prison!"

During his rant, Sophie dug behind her, latched onto the door handle and pulled. The door flew open on his last word and she fell out backward, hit the asphalt and rolled. The bullet shattered the passenger-door window. The bullet he'd meant for her head.

Claude dove across the seat, grasping for her even as she struggled to find some balance and get her feet under her. His hand latched onto her ankle, throwing her off, and she kicked out blindly with her other foot.

Her heel caught the hand with the gun and the weapon tumbled to the ground. She started to reach for it, but Claude was already coming at her fast. Her hand swiped the weapon, sending it into a nearby bush. She gave a hard yank with her captured foot and found herself free. Rolling and scrambling to get away from him, she lurched to her feet.

Only to have him catch up to her and bring her back down hard. The breath whooshed from her lungs, stunning her into stillness.

"Where is she?"

"The chopper's searching, Luke," Gavin assured him. He'd been the first one to respond to Luke's call for help, pulling up thirty seconds after Luke had watched Sophie's kidnapper peel away from the curb.

Too late. He was going to be too late once again and someone he loved was going to die. Bruno whined in the back and Gavin's Tommy barked. "I shouldn't have left her alone. So stupid. What was I thinking?"

"I should have been there when you got there," Gavin said.

"No, I shouldn't have left her alone."

"You thought someone was out in the backyard. You went to investigate—something any and all of us would have done. Quit beating yourself up about it."

Easy for him to say. "It was a distraction," he muttered. "And I fell for it."

"We're going to find her."

The radio crackled, and Luke heard chopper blades then the pilot. "Location established. Willow Lake, Flushing Meadow Park. Eyes on the vehicle."

He gave the location and Luke released a joyous breath. "Go, go. We're not too far from there."

"Suspect and victim on the ground. Victim is running." The pilot kept up the report while Gavin screamed down the highway, dodging vehicles that were slow to pull over. Other officers fell in behind them, blue lights whirling. "Run, Sophie, run."

"Victim caught. Victim is being dragged toward the lake."

He was going to drown her.

Luke's heart pounded with enough force that he thought it might rupture. Prayers whispered from his lips. *Please, God, don't let me be too late. Not this time.*

SIXTEEN

Sophie yanked against his hold but found she just didn't have the strength. "I don't want to die!"

"Too bad! I'm not going back to prison and you're the only one who can send me there!"

Water reached her ankles, then her calves.

Absently, she noted the helicopter above. The spotlight shone down, illuminating them. "Police! Let her go!"

Claude screamed and pulled her farther into the frigid water. Sophie swung her elbow and connected with his temple. He stumbled and fell with a splash.

Pulse-pounding desperation sent her stumbling away back toward shore. She allowed herself a brief flicker of hope that she might actually get away.

Only to have that hope snuffed when a hand grasped her hair and yanked her backward. She went down. Under. She flailed, kicked and caught him in the stomach. For a brief second, his grip loosened and she surfaced long enough to fill her lungs with air and note the approaching sirens before he managed to get a better grip and dunk her back under.

Help was so close, but would she be able to fight him off long enough to allow them the time to reach her?

Frantic, her mind scrambled for a way to get loose while her hands reached, grasping for anything. Her fingers pried at his, but she gave that up almost immediately. He was too strong, and she was tiring quickly.

Her lungs screamed, her limbs grew heavy, sluggish.

God! Help me!

Bright lights flashed, then everything went black.

"Sophie!" Luke threw himself out of the vehicle before Gavin brought it to a stop. Bruno loped after him. Passed him and bolted into the water. Luke caught up and flung himself into the water where he'd seen Sophie go under. The man who'd held her was scrambling out of the water along the shore. "Go after him!"

Gavin's engine roared and he took off after the fleeing man. Bruno swam in circles. Indicating that was where Sophie was?

Other cruisers pulled in as Luke dove into the cold water. Frantic, he swam down, arms reaching, while he begged God to spare her. His fingers brushed something.

Hair?

Clothing?

Then nothing.

The seconds ticked past. A minute. A minute and a half.

He surfaced, gasped in another lungful of air, noticed Bruno had moved and was swimming in circles a yard away. Luke went back down and kicked over to Bruno. Visibility was at absolute zero in the dark murkiness.

Then something bumped his leg.

He spun and shot out his hands. His palms grazed cold, smooth skin. Luke grasped hair and pulled. It had to be Sophie. He maneuvered her until he had her in a lifeguard hold and kicked to the surface.

Thankfully, the water wasn't deep and his feet hit bottom. He lifted her face and turned her toward him.

"Over here!" Zach called to him.

An ambulance was working its way toward them, but Luke wasn't about to wait on them. Sophie needed to breathe.

He stumbled out of the water and dropped to his knees, placing her on the ground. He felt for a pulse and found it, but she wasn't breathing.

Luke tilted her head and opened her mouth. He

leaned down to give her the breath from his lungs. Once, twice, three times.

Nothing.

Vaguely aware of the paramedics dropping beside him, he continued to breathe for her.

Until she gasped, then choked.

Luke rolled her on her side as she gave up the water she'd inhaled. When her body calmed after one final shudder, he rolled her back, and she stared up at him. Her eyes filled with tears.

"Thank you," she whispered. "I knew you'd come." Her eyes shut, and someone nudged him aside.

"Good job," a voice said from behind him. "We've got her now."

Luke fell back and let the paramedics take over. The shakes hit him—from the combination of crashing adrenaline and being soaking wet, no doubt—and he clasped his hands together, but he'd done it. He'd gotten to her on time. Barely. But she was alive. "Thank you, God," he whispered. "Thank you." Bruno nudged him and Luke wrapped an arm around the wet dog and slipped him his favorite toy in reward. "Good job, boy. You helped me save her."

Once the paramedics made sure she was stable, one of them tossed Luke a blanket and he wrapped it around his shoulders. He used a second blanket to rub down Bruno.

"You okay?" the guy asked.

"Yes." Luke shivered, and Bruno shook himself, spraying the remaining droplets. "Is she?"

"She will be once we get her warmed up and all of the water out of her lungs." He turned back to help his partner move her onto the gurney, then they carried her up the slight hill and loaded her into the ambulance.

Luke followed, not wanting to leave her side. He turned to Zach. "Give Bruno and me a ride?"

"Of course."

"I need to call Sophie's dad. He'll want to be there for her. I left my phone and weapon in Gavin's vehicle."

Zach handed his phone over.

It only took Luke a few seconds to get the man's number and give him a condensed version of the events that led to Sophie being taken to the hospital.

"I'm on the way," Sophie's father said. "You're sure she's all right?"

"She will be."

"Thank you." Luke heard the slamming of a car door just as he hung up.

Luke climbed in the passenger seat of Zach's Tahoe and ran a hand over his wet head and buckled up. He then used Zach's phone to make arrangements for his roommate David to take care of Bruno, grab him some clothes and meet them at the hospital. Then he dialed Gavin.

"You get him?" Luke asked when the man answered.

"No. I didn't, but a car did. He ran into the highway and got hit by a passing motorist. He's dead and the guy who hit him is a basket case." The weariness in his team member's voice said he wasn't happy. "He's the one who tried to get to Sophie the day of the funeral."

"Yes—and kidnapped her from the auditorium."

"Did he kill Jordan?"

"I don't know," Luke said. "Hopefully, Sophie can fill us in when she wakes up. The lab report came back on the content of the syringe. Let's just say if Jenks had managed to inject her, she would be dead."

"I'm glad she's okay."

"Same here."

"I'm on the way to the hospital," Gavin said.

"I think everyone is. See you there."

Zach dropped Luke at the door and Luke hurried to find Sophie. She was still in the emergency department. He flashed his badge and made his way to her side.

A man he'd never seen before sat in the chair next to her bed holding her hand. Sophie's father was his first guess. The man looked up when Luke stepped into the room. "Hi. I'm Luke Hathaway."

The man stood. "Damien Walters."

They shook hands and Luke stepped over to Sophie's side. "Has she woken up yet?"

"I think they have her on a painkiller. The guy knocked her around pretty good." Rage flashed on his features for a moment before he focused back on his daughter. "She briefly opened her eyes about a minute after I got here. Long enough to tell me not to worry," Mr. Walters said, his voice rough with emotion.

"That sounds like Sophie," Luke said. He gripped her other hand and squeezed.

Her eyes fluttered and finally opened and looked straight into his. "Luke?"

"Yeah."

"You saved me," she whispered.

His throat tightened. "Couldn't have done it without some help, but yeah."

"You weren't too late."

He gave a strangled laugh. "No, not this time." But it had definitely been close. Way too close. If he'd been only seconds later...

He shuddered as the nightmare of his mother's murder swept over him.

"Did you get him?" she whispered. "His name is Claude Jenks. He knows who killed Jordan."

Luke stilled. "It wasn't him?"

"Jenks said he didn't kill anyone. He insisted he was simply hired by someone. I got the feeling he was telling the truth."

"Who hired him?"

"I don't know. He wouldn't tell me. He said he was just supposed to put the envelope in Jordan's folder before the graduation ceremony and leave." She closed her eyes and sighed. "I'm sorry. I tried to get him to tell me once I realized he didn't actually kill Jordan himself."

"You don't have anything to apologize for," Luke said. "You just rest and focus on getting better."

"Okay." Her eyes closed and he started to leave when her grip tightened. "Don't leave me," she whispered without opening her eyes.

Luke's heart trembled, then fell over the edge right into love. He sighed as he tried to stop the acknowledgment. "I'm not going anywhere." For now. Again, memories from his childhood swept over him. His mother's bleeding body on the asphalt. Her funeral. His father's withdrawal and his brothers' accusing eyes. *You should have been on time! Why weren't you on time?*

His father's words echoed, and he kept his head down while he grappled with the memories.

When Sophie's breathing evened out, Luke looked up and his gaze connected with Mr. Walters.

The man's lips curved into a slow smile. "I think I'll go get something to eat. You'll let me know if she needs anything?"

"Of course."

"You're in love with her."

"We're...friends," Luke said with a quick glance at the, thankfully, still-sleeping Sophie.

Her father frowned, then nodded and headed for the door, stopping to clap Luke on the shoulder. "Thank you for saving my little girl." And then he was gone.

But his words lingered. *You love her.* Yes, he did. He hadn't intended to, but she'd sneaked her way into his heart and Luke clung to the fact that this incredible woman loved him. He knew she did but was afraid to admit it. He didn't blame her.

Luke pressed fingers to his weary eyes but couldn't help the small laugh of relief that broke through. Sophie was alive and her would-be killer dead.

The smile faded as reality set in. And he was going to have to figure out how to walk away from the woman he'd just admitted he loved.

SEVENTEEN

The next day when Sophie woke, she took a physical inventory and she decided her lungs were much clearer and, while she was sore, she would recover without any permanent side effects.

"Hi," Katie said.

Sophie turned to see her friend sitting in the chair. "Hi."

"How are you feeling?"

"Much better." She maneuvered herself into a sitting position. "How about you?"

"Sick, but the doctor said the baby's fine."

"I'm glad. Have you told the others?"

"No." Katie sighed. "But it's time. I've decided this baby is a huge blessing. Everyone will be excited that a little piece of Jordan will live on and…" She shook her head as tears filled her eyes.

"Sad that he won't be here to watch him grow up?"

Katie nodded and swiped her cheeks. "But," she said, "this baby will have lots of father figures in his or her life and will grow up knowing how much Jordan would have loved him. Or her."

"You're so right. And you know Ellie's going to want to be a little mama to her cousin."

Katie laughed. "Oh yes, for sure."

Sophie squeezed her friend's hand. "It's going to be okay, eventually, right?"

"Yes. Jordy would want us to be okay. So, we have to be. For him—and us, too. It's going to be a process, but I have to believe it."

"Yeah," Sophie said, "I'm believing it, too."

Fifteen minutes later, Noah, Luke, Zach and Carter gathered around her bed. After Sophie assured them she was fine and would be going home later that day, she turned the conversation to a question that burned in her mind. "You weren't able to find anything that might tell you the relationship between Claude Jenks and Jordan, were you?"

"Not yet," Zach said, "but we will."

"Did he tell you who killed Jordan?"

The brothers and Luke exchanged a look. "What?" she asked.

"When Jenks was running to get away from you, he ran into the path of a car and was killed."

Sophie gasped. "Then he couldn't tell you," she whispered.

"No, but the lab has everything that was on Jenks when he died," Luke said. "Although it looks like there wasn't anything salvageable, thanks to the water."

Carter ran a hand down his cheek. "We searched his home but found nothing to indicate who hired him to leave the note." The man shook his head. Weariness and grief were still deeply etched on his face and Sophie swallowed the lump that formed in her throat. She had a feeling she'd be doing a lot of that over the next few months.

With a nod, she glanced at Luke, who shot her a stiff smile. Sophie's heart ached. While he'd stayed right by her side, she could feel him pulling away emotionally.

"We'll get him," she said to the brothers. "We will."

"There's no other option," Carter said. His brothers nodded, jaws like granite, eyes narrowed. They all looked so very much alike at the moment, their expressions very similar to one she'd seen on Jordan's face more than once.

"We're going to go," Katie said. She rose. "You need to rest so you can get out of here."

"Thank you." Sophie's gaze swept across them. "I would be dead without you. I want you to know how grateful I am."

Each one patted her shoulder as they left the room, with Katie swooping in for another hug. "Rest."

Sophie's eyes landed on Luke, who was edging toward the door. "I will."

Katie left, and Sophie caught Luke's hand as he passed her. He stopped and raised a brow.

"What's wrong?" she asked.

His gaze slid away. "What do you mean?"

"You've never been evasive with me before. Don't start now."

Luke sucked in a deep breath and pulled his hand from hers to pace to the window. He looked out. "I'm dealing with some pretty raw emotions right now."

"Care to share?"

He raked a hand over his hair, then spun to face her, the torment in his eyes stabbing her heart. "I failed you, and I'm sorry."

Sophie huffed in disbelief. "*Failed* me? How can you even think that? You *saved* me."

"But I almost didn't. I let Bruno's barking distract me when I should have been on high alert."

"I'll take almost, Luke. I'm alive and very happy to be so. It wasn't your fault. Just like it wasn't your fault that someone made the choice to carjack and kill your mother. We all have choices in life. Claude Jenks made his, whoever killed Jordan made his. Now you have to make yours."

His jaw worked, and he drew in a deep breath. "I'm sorry, but I just... I don't deserve you, Sophie." He pressed his fingers to his eyes and slipped out the door just as her father stepped inside. Luke nodded a greeting but didn't stop.

Her dad raised a brow. "Am I interrupting something?"

A tear slid down her cheek, and she swiped it away. "No. Apparently not." She drew in a deep breath. "But it's probably better this way."

"What way?"

She gave a light shrug. "I don't need to make any commitments right now. Not...yet. Dating Luke would make things really hard."

"Because you think you have to take care of Trey and me? That we can't survive without you?"

Her eyes locked on his. "What do you mean? Of course I don't think that."

"I think you do."

Yes, she probably did. "I love you and Trey, Dad. I do what I do because of that. And if I don't do it, who will?"

"Sophie, I think it's time I told you something."

She blinked. "What's that?"

"I can do laundry, honey. I can also cook."

She paused. "You can?"

"I can."

"Then why...?"

"Haven't I?"

"Um...yes."

"Because you seemed to need to do it. To heal. If you recall, I tried to get you to stop doing stuff after your mom left and it made things worse for you."

She vaguely remembered that.

"It's not that we don't need you," he said, "but we'll be okay. Besides, Trey's going to be gone in a few weeks anyway. I'm proud of him. He's reaching out and grabbing life by the horns. It's time for you to do the same." Sophie figured her jaw was inches from the mattress. He patted her leg and laughed. "I sound like I don't expect to ever see you again." A sigh slipped from him. "I just want you to be happy. Luke's a good man. I hope you two can work it out."

Tears hovered on her lashes and she blinked and shook her head. "I don't think he wants me anymore," she whispered.

"Oh, honey, I think he does. Just give him a little time to process some things."

Time. Well, she definitely had time.

Luke wasn't sure how long he stood outside of Sophie's hospital room with his eyes shut and his mind spinning. Had he just done that? He was an idiot letting his fear control him. But…he honestly believed what he said. He *didn't* deserve Sophie. She deserved better.

But there was no doubt he'd just hurt her terribly. He turned and placed a hand back on the handle and debated about apologizing. Then let go with a heavy sigh. No. He'd done the right thing.

Then why did he feel so awful?

Luke hurried to the elevator, calling himself all kinds of a coward. But he needed to think.

Outside the hospital, he climbed into the SUV and caught Bruno's gaze on him in the rearview mirror. Even the dog looked sad. Or maybe disappointed in Luke.

"Stop. It's best this way."

Bruno huffed a sigh and lay down.

Luke cranked the SUV and headed away while his heart beat heavy with regret. Without thinking about it, he drove to Griffin's. He could drown his sorrows in his coffee. Or a milkshake and a burger.

Leaving Bruno in the Tahoe, he went inside and grabbed a seat at the bar area. Violet Griffin was the only one around and she approached him with a smile. "Hi, Luke, how's it going?"

"Fine."

"You need to work on that."

"What?"

"Being convincing."

He grimaced. "I've got a lot on my mind right now."

"Jordan?"

"Among other things."

"Well, if you want to talk about it, I'm a good listener."

"That's okay, I'll work it out. Could I get a cup of coffee?"

"Black?"

"Yep."

"Coming up." A minute later, she set the steaming mug in front of him.

"Thanks."

"Sure. Could I ask you a question?"

"Go for it."

She paused, then sighed. "Do you think you'll ever figure out what happened to Jordy?"

He closed his eyes at the pain the question produced but nodded. "Yeah. I do."

"You know my parents live next door to the Jamesons, right?"

"Yes." He'd forgotten it until she just mentioned it, but he'd known that.

"My mom talks to Mrs. Jameson quite a bit. They're all blindsided and reeling."

"We all are."

"I don't think Zach's handling this very well."

"What do you mean?"

She shrugged. "Just a feeling I get. He comes in occasionally and just stares out the window. I'm worried about him."

So she'd said before. "You seem to be mostly focused on Zach. Is there something else going on?"

A flush crept into her cheeks. "No, of course not. All the Jamesons are like family. It's just… Zach seems to be taking it the hardest, that's all."

"I'll keep an eye on him," Luke said softly. He hadn't noticed, but maybe that was because he'd been so lost in his own grief and roller-coaster emotions when it came to Sophie that he just hadn't been aware.

"That would be great, Luke. Can I get you anything else? I've got to take off in a bit for a shift at the airport."

"I'm all right for now but thank you."

"Okay. Mom and Dad are both in the back if you need anything." She swept the apron over her head and disappeared into the kitchen.

Luke sipped his coffee and decided Violet wasn't completely truthful with him. When he'd first met her, he'd thought she and Zach were a couple because of the way they went back and forth with each other. Sniping about nothing, grumbling like an old married couple.

When Violet headed for the door a few minutes later, he turned. "Hey, Violet?"

She stopped at the door and glanced back at him. "Yes?"

"Why haven't you and Zach ever gotten together?"

This time the flush darkened her cheeks to a deep red. "I don't know what you're talking about." And then she was gone.

He smirked. Right.

His mirth faded immediately, and he finished his coffee as he continued to second-guess himself. His mind knew Sophie was right. It wasn't his fault his mother was dead. It wasn't his fault

Claude Jenks had almost killed Sophie. And it wasn't his fault that Jordan was dead because he hadn't found him in time. His heart wanted to argue.

Luke grabbed his keys and left the diner, heading home with Bruno. When he came to his front door, he noted it had been fixed temporarily and wondered who he had to thank for that. Probably one of his unit members. Gratitude swept over him even as the empty house slapped him in the face.

Never before Sophie had he minded coming home to the emptiness. Now he wanted her here.

Bruno whined and headed and down the hall to Sam's room. "She's not here, boy."

The dog kept going. When he came back, he slumped onto his bed in front of the fireplace, eyeing Luke with the demand that he fix this.

Luke dropped onto the couch and decided to pray about the big hole in the vicinity of his heart that he had a feeling only Sophie could fill.

When Sophie walked into the office two days later, she had a smile on her face in spite of the heaviness in her heart. Her father had asked her to stay upstairs with him her first night home from the hospital and she'd agreed but couldn't stand his well-meant hovering and sad, knowing eyes.

"It's about that man who wouldn't leave your side, isn't it?" her father had asked.

"What?"

"Luke. He's the deep sadness you can't hide."

"Yes. It's about him, but I don't want to talk about it because there's nothing to say, okay? He made his choice and I'll heal. And besides, a romance wouldn't work now anyway."

"Why not?"

"Because I've just got too much going on right now."

"Meaning me and Trey?"

She'd blinked. "Well, no. I mean—"

"Honey, Trey and I love all that you do for us, but we can't be your life. You need to go after what you want. What you need. Don't let us stand in your way of a future full of happiness."

"You're not." But Luke was.

Her father had hugged her and kissed the top of her head and that had been the end of it.

Except for the *looks*.

So, she'd gone downstairs to her place to escape. And been miserably lonely with only her thoughts to keep her company.

This morning, she'd rolled out of bed after a restless sleep filled with nightmares of drowning and headed to the office, determined to get her mind off her troubles.

She walked through the lobby toward her office and waved to Zach, whose desk was closest to her door. He stood. "Hey, everyone, Sophie's back!"

A cheer went up and clapping started. Everyone

was in the office today. Bree, Gavin, Reed, Tony, the Jameson brothers and Finn were on their feet.

After a long round of applause, Sophie pressed her hands to her heated cheeks. "Thanks, guys. You sure know how to embarrass a girl." But they knew she loved their show of appreciation.

However, she couldn't help but notice Luke wasn't there.

Noah stepped out of Jordan's old office. "Welcome back, Sophie. This place hasn't been the same without you." He hugged her and some of her sadness lifted. It was nice to be missed.

"I'm glad to be back, thanks."

He looked down at her, concern drawing his brows together. "You know, no one would fault you for needing to take more time. You've been through a huge trauma."

She shook her head. "I'm not going anywhere. This is my home and you guys are my family." Even if staying meant seeing Luke every day. Things would never be the same between them— and maybe that was one of the reasons she wanted to stay. She hadn't quite given up hope that he would eventually come around and realize he could love her in spite of his past.

"Good," Noah said, "I'm glad we've got that settled."

The door opened, and Katie stepped inside. Her right hand rested lightly on her abdomen and Sophie thought she caught a hint of tears in her eyes before she took a deep breath. "Hi, guys."

Everyone stopped. Noah went to his sister-in-law and gave her a hug. "What are you doing here?"

"I came to pick up some of Jordan's things, and—"

"And?"

"I also came to tell you all something since you're here."

The others gathered closer. Carter raised a brow and threw an arm across Zach's shoulders. "Everything okay?"

Katie met Sophie's gaze. Sophie smiled her encouragement.

"I've already told your parents and they told me I had to get down here ASAP and tell you."

The brothers exchanged frowns. "Katie—"

She held up a hand and Noah fell silent. "Let me finish, please." Her gaze swept the room, touching on all of them. "I just noticed Luke isn't here."

"He'll be here soon," Sophie said. "But it's okay. Go ahead."

Katie cleared her throat and Zach groaned. "Come on, Katie, spill it."

"I am, I promise. I just wanted to say how much I love all of you and how grateful I am that I got to be married to Jordan."

Sophie's throat closed and from the sudden silence, she figured hers wasn't the only one.

"Anyway," Katie said, "I know we've all been terribly sad, but I've got some good news."

The tension in the room lightened considerably.

"The day Jordan disappeared, we had an appointment that was supposed to take place after the graduation ceremony. Unfortunately, that never happened." She drew in a deep breath and blinked back the tears that surged in her pretty blue eyes. "Anyway, I just wanted to let you all know that Jordan will live on in his son or daughter." The last word slipped out on a whisper.

Sophie swiped a tear that insisted on leaking down her cheek.

Zach cleared his throat. "Aw, Katie, that's… that's…" He couldn't finish his thought due to the emotions obviously overwhelming him. Sophie stepped forward and gripped his arm.

Carter let out a whoop. "What my brother's trying to say is that's fabulous." He hugged her, and Katie let out a teary laugh.

One by one, the others congratulated and hugged her and Sophie could see how much the news meant to Jordan's brothers.

"Hey, everyone," Bree said, "not to steal Katie's thunder, but I just got a text from Ynez. Stella's had her puppies! I'm going to go see them. Is that okay, Noah?"

Ynez Dubois, the vet they used whenever they needed one.

Noah shook his head and laughed. "Sure, why not? Who can resist puppies?"

Sophie could tell he'd agreed because he knew they all needed all the lighthearted, feel-good moments they could get right now.

"I know it's not nearly as exciting as Katie being pregnant," Bree said, "but babies are babies, right?"

"Right," Sophie said. Together, they walked the short distance from the offices to the vet's.

Dr. Ynez Dubois met them at the door. "Wow, the whole crew is here. Follow me."

Sophie held back and let the others go first. She wanted to see the pups, but Luke's absence put a damper on her joy.

And then it was her turn to kneel next to the sleeping bundles of yellow, brown and black. "They're so precious."

"They're going to need homes when they're big enough," Dr. Dubois said. Her lightly accented voice held a world of hope. "Any of you up for fostering?"

Sophie looked up at her and smiled. "I am." She could use the company. And if the pup eventually was deemed able to be trained for the NYPD, then she would get to see the dog on a regular basis. If, for some reason, its temperament wasn't compatible with K-9 work, then she'd have a pet. A win-win situation in her opinion.

"Hey, everyone, I heard a rumor that we've got

some new additions that'll be ready for training before too long."

Sophie froze at the sound of Luke's voice.

"Come take a look," Gavin said.

Luke stepped up next to her and Sophie's breath caught. He looked tired, but...peaceful?

"I'm surprised to see you here," he said to her as Bruno shouldered his way to her and nudged her with his snout.

She shrugged and scratched Bruno's head until he seemed satisfied with the attention and moved on to the area where the puppies were. After a brief sniff of the tiny bodies, at Stella's low growl, he turned and walked to the far corner of the room, where he lay down.

Sophie looked back at the puppies, not wanting Luke to see the hurt—and longing—in her eyes. "I've got work to do."

"Like what?"

"Like resend some emails to all the shelters and parks department staff to remind them Snapper's still missing. Gotta stay on top of things, you know?" She was babbling. Not that it wasn't true, but... She sighed. "Staying at home produces nothing but tears. I just...need to work." She stayed on her knees, hoping Luke would take the hint and move on.

EIGHTEEN

Luke swallowed hard. He'd made up his mind about what he was going to do when he saw her again, but her cold shoulder sent his anxiety soaring—along with his determination. Nope, he wasn't going to wimp out. And he wasn't going to live his life in fear or self-blame. He drew in a deep breath and knelt beside her. "Hey, would you want to take a walk?" he whispered.

This time she met his gaze, startled. "Now?"

"Yes, please?"

She gave the nearest puppy's head a gentle scratch. "Where?"

"Back to headquarters, I guess." He glanced at the others still enamored with the pups and light-heartedly arguing which ones would be trained in what specialty. "While everyone else is otherwise occupied?"

"Um…okay. Why?"

"Because I want to talk to you and I don't need

a nosy audience. If we're careful, I think we can slip out without being noticed."

"They can be a nosy bunch, can't they?" She offered him a small smile.

He took her hand and breathed easier when she didn't pull away from him. He helped her to her feet, gathered Bruno's leash and led her out the door. The dog trailed along a few steps behind, content just to be with them.

"I decided to take a lesson from Bruno—and you," Luke said.

"What kind of lesson?"

"Look at him. He works hard, he's good at what he does, but he knows how to chill and enjoy life. I want to be like that."

"Okay."

He laughed and shook his head. "You're not going to make this easy, are you?"

Her eyes softened. "I'm not trying to make it difficult, Luke. I just need you to tell me what you're thinking."

"I'm thinking you were right."

A smile started to curve her lips. "About?"

"You know what about." He sighed. "I really messed things up with you and I'm sorry. I was very wishy-washy and inconsistent. You didn't deserve that."

"Thank you."

"I know what I want, Sophie, I'm just praying you want it, too."

"What's that?"

"A future together. Honestly, Sophie, every time I look at my future, you're in it. If I try to picture it without you, well, it's just not possible."

Tears flooded her eyes. "I thought you didn't want to pursue anything between us until Jordan's killer was found. What's changed?"

He gave a slow nod. "That's a fair question." He paused, wanting, needing to find the right words. "I didn't think I'd ever find someone I could trust my heart with again. Not after it took such a beating, but then you came along and the attraction I felt—and I think you felt—scared me. I think I was using the case to protect myself from my feelings for you. In other words, I was running like a coward."

"You're not a coward."

"Thanks."

"What kind of feelings?"

He huffed a short chuckle, then sucked in a deep breath. "Sophie, I'm not good at expressing myself. I never have been. After my mom was killed, I sort of locked everything up inside because I'd decided feelings were bad. Not all, of course, but you couldn't have the good without the bad, so I just decided not to feel."

"It was your coping mechanism. You were protecting yourself."

"Maybe." He sighed. "Probably. And the truth is, sometimes it worked, sometimes it didn't. With you, it didn't. I started falling in love with you the minute Jenks shoved you into my arms and we fell on the sidewalk."

She gave a breathless puff of laughter. "What?"

"And you popped up like you weren't hurting and said we needed to get back to headquarters. You were so spunky and determined and… I realized I was in trouble from that moment on."

"Trouble, hmm?"

"Well, my heart anyway. And then when you were kidnapped and I almost didn't get there in time…" He looked away and drew in yet another breath, steadying his emotions. "Walking away from you in the hospital was one of the hardest things I've ever done…and one of the dumbest."

"I'm glad you realize that last part."

He laughed. "I guess what I'm trying to say in my bumbling, awkward way is that life is short. Too short not to grab hold of something when it's right. And I think you and I together are very, very right."

Sophie couldn't stop the tears from falling any more than she could stop the tide from coming in. "You really think it's right?"

"Yes. I really do. I've come to the conclusion that age is just a number. Everyone is different and I was silly to judge you based on a number. You're so very…you. Young, but much older than I am in a lot of ways."

"Because of the way I grew up, probably. I had a lot of responsibility on my shoulders and had to grow up fast. Just like you did, if you think about it."

"Maybe. All I know is that I couldn't stand it if I lost you, Sophie."

She sniffed and swiped a hand across her cheek. "You're not going to lose me."

"But that's my point. We don't know what the future holds, and I don't want to waste another minute of it *fearing* it, being afraid to trust again and take chances. I want to live boldly and face it with you. Together. Um…you and me. Us."

"Luke?"

"Yes?"

"Could you just say it, please?"

"I love you, Sophie."

"Thank you."

He blinked. "Thank you? That's it?"

"And I love you, too. I think I have for a long time."

"What do you mean?"

"I mean, I noticed you when you weren't noticing me."

"But…you never said anything."

She scoffed. "Of course not. What was I going to do, walk up to you and ask you out and have you say, 'Who are you again?'"

"I wasn't *that* bad!"

She grinned. "Almost." Then sobered. "And

I was worried about my dad and brother." She gave a short self-deprecating laugh. "Apparently, they don't need me quite as much as I thought they did."

"They need you. Just maybe not in the ways you thought."

"I know. Dad made that pretty clear." She paused. "Is it bad to be so happy while Jordan's killer is still out there?"

"What do you think?"

A slow smile slipped across her lips. "I think he'd be thrilled for us."

"Absolutely. And super mad at us if we don't cherish what we've got."

Sophie nodded, hard-pressed to get any more words past her tight throat. Jordan had lived each day with full gusto, determined to make the world a better place before he died. And he'd done that by investing in the lives of those he came into contact with.

"I don't want to be your coworker anymore," Luke said, his voice husky with emotion.

"You don't?" she squeaked. "Well, why not?"

"Because I want to be your husband. If that's okay with you."

With a squeal, Sophie launched herself into Luke's arms and planted a serious kiss on his surprised lips. He laughed when she came up for air. "Is that a yes?"

"That's a definite yes."

Cheers erupted from behind them and Luke spun, Sophie still in his arms. Sophie giggled at the sight that greeted her. Every last team member stood gawking and clapping.

"Way to go, Luke!" Zach pumped a fist in the air and Luke grinned at him. "It's about time you opened your eyes and saw the woman was crazy about you."

"He knew?"

"Everybody in the office probably did," she admitted.

"Then I'd say it's definitely about time," he murmured.

Bruno barked twice.

Luke laughed. "I guess Bruno agrees."

"I agree with Bruno," she said. "Now, kiss me again. I've been waiting a long time for you to do so without an apology attached at the end."

So, he did.

* * * * *

If you enjoyed Justice Mission,
look for Zach and Violet's story,
Act of Valor,
*and the rest of the True Blue K-9 Unit series
from Love Inspired Suspense.*

*True Blue K-9 Unit:
These police officers fight for justice
with the help of their brave canine partners*

Dear Reader,

Welcome to the exciting world of the NYPD! I'm so happy to have you along for the series. Yes, I know you all want to know who killed Chief Jordan Jameson and that will be revealed later in this continuity. In the meantime, I hope you'll stay on the journey with us as each book takes you into the lives of the other heroes and heroines and their four-legged partners.

As you may have noticed, Luke Hathaway judged Sophie Walters by her appearance. Because he'd had a bad experience in the past, he was determined to guard his heart against another one. Which may be understandable. However, once he got to know Sophie, he realized exactly what he'd been missing out on. Thank goodness he let Sophie past the barriers he'd thrown up. Actually, now that I think about it, I'm not so sure he let her past them. I think she pretty much tore them down! Well, either way, I love that they wound up together and I look forward to catching up with them as the series unfolds.

Again, thank you for reading the books. We appreciate you very much!

God bless,
Lynette Eason

Get 4 FREE REWARDS!

We'll send you 2 FREE Books <u>plus</u> 2 FREE Mystery Gifts.

Harlequin® Heartwarming™ Larger-Print books feature traditional values of home, family, community and—most of all—love.

FREE Value Over $20

YES! Please send me 2 FREE Harlequin® Heartwarming™ Larger-Print novels and my 2 FREE mystery gifts (gifts worth about $10 retail). After receiving them, if I don't wish to receive any more books, I can return the shipping statement marked "cancel." If I don't cancel, I will receive 4 brand-new larger-print novels every month and be billed just $5.49 per book in the U.S. or $6.24 per book in Canada. That's a savings of at least 19% off the cover price. It's quite a bargain! Shipping and handling is just 50¢ per book in the U.S. and 75¢ per book in Canada.* I understand that accepting the 2 free books and gifts places me under no obligation to buy anything. I can always return a shipment and cancel at any time. The free books and gifts are mine to keep no matter what I decide.

161/361 IDN GMY3

Name (please print)

Address   Apt. #

City   State/Province   Zip/Postal Code

> Mail to the **Reader Service:**
> **IN U.S.A.:** P.O. Box 1341, Buffalo, NY 14240-8531
> **IN CANADA:** P.O. Box 603, Fort Erie, Ontario L2A 5X3

Want to try 2 free books from another series? Call 1-800-873-8635 or visit www.ReaderService.com.

---

*Terms and prices subject to change without notice. Prices do not include sales taxes, which will be charged (if applicable) based on your state or country of residence. Canadian residents will be charged applicable taxes. Offer not valid in Quebec. This offer is limited to one order per household. Books received may not be as shown. Not valid for current subscribers to Harlequin Heartwarming Larger-Print books. All orders subject to approval. Credit or debit balances in a customer's account(s) may be offset by any other outstanding balance owed by or to the customer. Please allow 4 to 6 weeks for delivery. Offer available while quantities last.

Your Privacy—The Reader Service is committed to protecting your privacy. Our Privacy Policy is available online at www.ReaderService.com or upon request from the Reader Service. We make a portion of our mailing list available to reputable third parties that offer products we believe may interest you. If you prefer that we not exchange your name with third parties, or if you wish to clarify or modify your communication preferences, please visit us at www.ReaderService.com/consumerschoice or write to us at Reader Service Preference Service, P.O. Box 9062, Buffalo, NY 14240-9062. Include your complete name and address.

HW19R

THE FORTUNES OF TEXAS COLLECTION!

Treat yourself to the rich legacy of the Fortune and Mendoza clans in this remarkable 50-book collection. This collection is packed with cowboys, tycoons and Texas-sized romances!